# MY LAST DATE

## RAISED BY WOLVES BOOK 5

## CASEY MORALES

Edited by
CARLIE SLATTERY

1

——————

**HAPPY TWO YEARS**

Ryan bounded down the stairs into the den. He wore little more than a broad grin and white cloth held together by a purple cord tied around his waist.

"What do you think?" He walked the length of our cozy den, turned, and struck a manly pose. "Roman enough?"

How did he manage to make his chest and arms look meaty in a makeshift toga? I swear his abs even poked through. Some people really had won the genetic lottery.

"You're a regular Caesar salad."

He grabbed a pillow off a chair and hurled it at me.

"Hey! No abusing the palace staff."

He laughed. "This is gonna be a blast. I've never done a murder mystery party before."

"Me either." I held up a thick binder. "I've been studying the case all afternoon. There are so many details I have to tell one character, but not another, and at seemingly random times I have to pass secret notes to players as they *discover* clues or hints. Most of those notes are cued off whatever crazy things the players say throughout the game. This narrator gig is real work."

He leaned down and gave me a peck on the cheek as he headed into the kitchen.

"You'll do great. You love telling stories," he called out between test bites of marinara. "Damn, this is really good, babe."

I'd started the made-from-scratch lasagna hours earlier, determined to let the sauce simmer for as long as possible before assembling the layers of Italian goodness. In addition to the traditional sauce, meat, cheeses, and pasta, I added mushrooms and spinach. This was one of Ryan's favorites and I wanted it to be perfect, both for him and the gaggle of gays about to assemble for our mystery mayhem.

---

THE PAST YEAR AND A HALF HAD PASSED SO QUICKLY.

During that time, we'd fully nested in our townhouse and established ourselves as a couple in the neighborhood. The lesbians across the street had latched onto us immediately, but others had approached with a bit more caution. There was a keen difference between living inside the gay bubble that was Midtown and living near it. We were clearly outside the cozy gay sanctuary, but close enough to feel its glow on our faces when we walked outside.

The relationship between Ryan and his ex, Diane, had evolved from confusion and bitterness into friendship and partnership. That had required time and countless hours of venting, crying, and a million questions anyone in her position would ask. I was so proud of how patient he'd been with her, but was even more impressed with her compassion and willingness to be open to the man who'd hurt her so deeply. It took such strength for her to accept this new person she was getting to know. At least, I guessed that's how it felt for her. We never spoke.

There were a few times Ryan came home exasperated by some of her questions. It reminded me of facing the inquisition by my parents every time I went home. I wanted to scream, "We've been over this a thousand times," but compassion drove me to follow a different path with those conversations. Ryan loved Diane, and she loved him. Their realities were intertwined, and only through love and understanding would their family survive and grow stronger.

Again, compassion reigned.

It's funny how often that word came to mind—and how critical it was for all of us.

Ryan and Diane remained a unified team in raising their kids, and while I didn't think she would ever truly understand Ryan's journey, she finally came to some healthy conclusions. She called one Saturday afternoon while we were cleaning the living room. I knew something was up, because Ryan's voice bounced from friendly to curious to concerned. He dropped his dusting rag and sat on the couch, staring into nothing, as she spoke. I continued cleaning the kitchen, trying not to hover—or, at least, to not *look like* I was hovering. Midway through the call, his tears began. I couldn't take it anymore, so I tossed my own rag and sat beside him, my arm around his quaking shoulder. I could just make out her voice in the receiver. She sounded strong, resolute, yet warm.

She started by announcing she now knew their divorce wasn't her fault. She hadn't done anything wrong and had given herself permission to stop blaming herself. It was the Mount Everest of emotional victories, and I was thrilled to hear her conquer that climb. To lose one's family and their white-picket-fence future was hard enough. Add a thick layer of guilt to the equation and anyone would suffocate under its weight. No one deserved that, especially not the mother of Ryan's children, a wonderful, caring woman who'd unfortunately married a man eighteen years before he fully knew himself.

She went on to tell Ryan to give himself a break, that their breakup wasn't his fault either. He was living his truth, and as painful as that might've been for all of them, she respected his courage to face it.

Alan and Elaine were growing up quickly. Ryan spent every other weekend with them at their house. Diane might've accepted Ryan, but she'd likely never accept me. As he put it, I represented everything that tore her marriage apart. Deep down, she didn't really believe I'd turned Ryan gay—like some rainbow-colored vampire with fairy dust dripping from my fangs—but for her, it was painful to think of me, the guy who now made Ryan smile. That had been her job for nearly two decades. As much as I wanted a relationship with the kids, I couldn't blame her for being protective of them—and of herself. She'd been through enough.

Ryan and I had become *that* couple. You know, the one others ogle over how they look at each other? That ogling came with admiration, a hint of jealousy, or the desire to visit the nearest dentist from the saccharine dripping from our mutual gaze.

Yeah, we were hopelessly in love.

Actually, that's inaccurate. We were hope*fully* in love.

Ryan wouldn't sleep without some part of us touching. Most nights we drifted off with my arm wrapped around him, our bodies pressed tightly together. His hands clutched mine until sleep overcame him. Even when the room was too hot to spoon, he pressed his toes against my leg. Somehow, we were always connected.

I'd never felt so safe, so loved.

And I'd never loved so freely and deeply.

In every prior relationship, I'd held a part of myself back, maintained that last wall to protect my heart in case things ended. The only exception prior to Ryan had been Carter, my first, and that was only because I had absolutely no clue what I was doing. After that gut-wrenching breakup, I vowed never to give up that last line of defense against heart-crushing pain.

Ryan made it past that wall.

He scaled it—or smashed through it, I'm not sure which.

I couldn't keep him out, and I didn't want to. A

little over a year into our relationship, I felt that defense crumble. We were on another of his work trips in San Francisco. He'd just locked me up in an Alcatraz cell, one of our favorite tourist destinations in Rice-a-Roni town. We laughed as we walked out of the prison. Other tourists glared and smiled at our silliness. The sun was setting on the bay. The breeze carried a tickling tang. As we reached the dock to board the ferry, he ignored the assembled masses and tenderly brushed the hair from my forehead. His gaze was intense, like peering into a bottomless well and finding no end to its depth. My breath caught when I looked into his eyes.

In that moment, I knew he was forever. He was *my* forever.

And the last wall fell.

IT FELT LIKE ONLY DAYS OR WEEKS AGO THAT RYAN and I had met for the first time in Caribou, then made a day of putt-putt. But it had been years. Two of them, to be precise. Time moved so fast.

This gathering was our way of including our closest friends in the anniversary celebration. We'd seen so many gay couples break up in recent months that we wanted to give encouragement to those giving a serious relationship a whirl. We wanted to show them that two men really *could* make it work.

Ryan took another bite before tossing his spoon in the dishwasher.

"Dinner's in good hands. I'm going upstairs to finish getting ready. Need me to do anything?"

"Mind setting the table? There are place cards with each character's name and a seating chart on the table. I need each player seated in specific order. Everyone's supposed to arrive in character, and stay in character until the game is over."

His brows rose. "Wow. You really have been working."

"Yep. Now, Caesar, out of my kitchen before I beat you with dried pasta."

"Don't threaten me with a good time, Brutus. A pasta beating sounds fun, especially if it's your big noodle doing the spanking." He swatted my butt and scurried out of the room, his toga fluttering dramatically behind.

I tried not to smile, but Ryan knew how to push my buttons.

God, I loved it when he pushed my…

Never mind.

**2**

———

## MURDER MYSTERY PARTY

Fin and Rob were the first to arrive. Rob wore a tight-fitting toga trimmed in purple; Fin was decked out in full Roman soldier regalia. The light of our lamps danced in the golden sheen of his breastplate, shin guards, and helmet. Atop the helmet was six inches of maroon plumes, marking him as a high-ranking officer. They had clearly visited a costume shop and were determined to be the evening's best-dressed guests.

"Hail Caesar!" Fin declared with a closed fist across his chest. He smacked it a little too hard and winced as he shook out his knuckles.

Rob and I giggled.

"Welcome, soldier. Who have you brought to my humble home?" I asked in character.

"May I present the Honorable Senator Velum

Pendulum." He motioned with his hand, then leaned over and whispered conspiratorially, "He swings both ways, if you get my meaning."

I spit a laugh. Rob rolled his eyes theatrically.

This was going to be a fun night. There was no one in town with a sharper wit—or dirtier mind —than Fin.

"It is an honor, Senator. Please, come in. Enjoy some refreshment. The others should arrive shortly."

I bowed and extended a palm toward the dining room table. Ryan had found an ancient-looking jug at an antique shop and had dutifully filled it with wine for the evening. The glasses were plastic goblets he'd found at a party store. Ryan was definitely feeling the spirit of our Roman adventure.

The Senator and his guard were pillaging the charcuterie as I walked back to the kitchen to check on the lasagna. Before I could lift the Magic Spoon of Goodness, the doorbell rang again.

"Coming. You two keep eating," I called out.

I pulled the door open to reveal the last of our murder mystery cast. Abe, the only player assigned to an opposite-gender role, gave us his best Miss America pageant wave, completely ignored me, and strode into the room with his chin held high enough to catch rainwater in his nose.

Where Fin and Rob were relatively masculine—at

least, relative to the more flamboyant of the gay species—Abe's flame burned brighter and more colorfully than the aurora borealis. He relished the opportunity to dress up and fan that flame. His foot-high blond Marge Simpson wig was paired with palm-sized, bangle-style clip-on earrings and a gaudy set of faux-gold neck chains. A silky cloth was wrapped around his waist, attempting to replicate a flowing white dress trimmed in gold. I'd seen that cloth on his dining room table not long ago. The faded mustard stain near his crotch gave it away.

Invoking the spirit of Monty Python, two halves of a coconut—the white meat still intact—covered his less-than-ample bosom, but did nothing to part the pelt of thick, wiry brown hair that blanketed his chest, shoulders, and back. Neon-pink lipstick was the icing on the very furry cake.

He looked like a Wookie with fruity boobs leaping out of a marshmallow.

"Hey, ya'll Roman hotties. The most voluptuous maiden the gods ever made has arrived. You may worship me now," he said in his most un-Roman accent.

Fin guffawed. Rob waved back with the floppy slice of salami he was holding.

"You know I love a man who knows how to wiggle his meat. Maybe I'll just sit in your lap all night, let you play with my coco-nips." He lifted his half-shells with his palms and tossed back his flowing hair.

Before I could react, Ryan appeared at the foot of the stairs. He'd added a wreath of golden leaves, apparently claiming the title of champion for his character. His arms bulged nicely out of his sheet-turned-toga, so I didn't call foul on his straying from the character sheet. After all, if coconuts were in play, who was I to question a few leaves on his head?

"How wonderful," Ryan opened his arms wide. "Our dearest friends together in our home. Oh, and you, Senator. You're here too, I see."

Ryan really was in character. His role, Flavius, absolutely hated Senator Sweet Cheeks, and wasn't shy about saying so. The good senator felt even more animosity toward the evening's host.

"Yes, Flavo, so good of you to invite me. Your home is so…quaint." He waved his salami about the room.

Satisfied the players were sticking to their scripts, I slipped out of the room to rescue the lasagna from the now-beeping oven. Ryan would never let me live it down if I burned his favorite dish on party night.

From the safety of the kitchen, I chuckled as everyone introduced their characters to the others. It was awkward at first, almost mechanical, as they recited lines from their character sheets. Ten minutes in, they'd caught the fever and were ad-libbing liberally and breathing life into their Roman alter-egos.

Flavius was stoic; the good senator grumbled and groused; while Gladius, our six-foot-four body-of-death Roman guard, let coconut-crusted Leesha nest in his lap and play flirtatiously with his plume.

---

IT TOOK OVER TWO HOURS TO MAKE IT THROUGH salad, lasagna, and tiramisu. When the fourth bottle of wine emitted that satisfying *pop* of a cork-pull, we skipped pouring its contents into the Roman jug and liberally refilled glasses around the table. Everyone stayed in character, but decanting the grape juice delayed the process of getting naughty Romans more drunk.

Hail Caesar!

The mystery revolved around a murder that had taken place the night before our gathering in the home of the host, Flavius. Each member of the cast was a suspect in some way, and the players' goal was to unmask the murderer with the information gleaned from the other players throughout dinner.

I stood and walked around the table, clearing the

last of the plates, and handed a sealed note to Gladius as I passed into the kitchen.

It read, *Last night, while you were on patrol around the manse, two voices pierced the darkness. One spoke of "eliminating" the poor murdered Roman, while the other grunted in agreement. The conversation cut off mid-sentence as you rounded a corner near where the speakers were hiding. You didn't see them, but think one of them was Flavius, the owner of the manse.*

We were getting down to the end. The clues were becoming pointed. What remained the most inter-esting mystery was how the players handled their information. These weren't seasoned actors, but they had to tie off loose ends while keeping their game face intact—or, in the case of Leesha, keeping her coconuts from falling off.

I looked back over my shoulder from the kitchen and caught Ryan staring at me. He smiled, and his eyes glittered in that way that told me I was the only man in his world. Two years into our relationship, his gaze still made my heart flutter.

I winked and disappeared into the kitchen, wondering if that gaze would change when he learned his beloved character, Flavius, was the murderer. A stage knife, complete with a squirter and vial of catsup, was prepared for his eventual execution.

His crime would forever be a stain on our house.

———

FIN DRAINED THE LAST DROPS OF WINE INTO HIS OPEN mouth, nearly hitting the ceiling fan as he tipped the bottle.

Tall people suck.

Ryan and Rob were dousing and scrubbing the catsup stain on Ryan's toga. His execution had been epic. Fin took great pleasure in drawing the faux knife across his neck and emptying every last drop of condiment onto his chest and lap. Red splattered more than it shot, coating him and the nearby dining room table. Abe giggled and applauded, using his best golf clap, the fingertips of one hand lightly tapping the meaty palm of the other in a most delicate and feminine way.

As he clapped and mocked the dearly departed, one coconut lost its grip and clanked to the floor.

Uni-boob was horrified.

I laughed so hard my side hurt, and I nearly piddled on the spot.

"How can you laugh at a lady in distress?" he squawked, hastily retrieving the half-shell that was rolling in lazy arcs across the floor.

"Blood and broken boobs. What could be funnier?" I quipped.

Rob sucked in a breath and looked up from his dabbing. "That gives me an idea."

He waited for us to settle and look at him.

*Oh shit.* He was up to something.

He turned to Ryan. "You and Michael should come to Decadence with us."

Ryan cocked his head at me. I shrugged, utterly lost.

"Decadence? The holiest of holy gay holidays?" Rob gaped. "You two are hopeless. Just say yes. We're renting a house just off Bourbon Street. All you need to do is book a flight and go shopping."

"Shopping?" Ryan asked.

Rob looked between Ryan and me with pity. "Oh, sweeties. Have you seen your wardrobe? You look like lesbians headed to Home Depot for fashion week. You'll need something much tighter, and preferably easily removed."

He winked up at Fin. The giant grinned conspiratorially.

Ryan looked to me again.

I shrugged again, nodding once. "Why not?"

"Awesome! It's in two weeks," Rob said. "Oh, one thing. You'll want to take a day off, the one after we get back. You might need to recover a bit."

**3**

---

## BREAD PUDDIN'

Ryan was in charge of travel for a large corporation. He negotiated preferred vendor arrangements with airlines, hotels, rental car companies, as well as a dozen other modes of travel or vital links in the moving-people chain. He had so many frequent flyer miles and free hotel nights that we rarely paid for travel or lodging.

Travel perks were seriously cool.

He turned toward me and leaned across the thick leather first-class recliner.

"So, babe. Do you have any idea what we're getting into down here? Rob had mischief in his voice when he invited us."

I snorted through my vodka-heavy Screwdriver. "Mischief? More like pure evil."

He grinned and raised a glass in salute. "What did Dwayne say about this trip? Did you tell Connie?"

"Oh yeah. Dwayne warned us away from dark corners. I asked if he'd been to a Decadence before, but he refused to answer. I'm pretty sure he's been a bad little boy in New Orleans at least once."

"And Connie?"

"She didn't really know what Decadence was. Just told us to have fun and stay safe. Oh, and to take pictures of any hotties we find. She's all about some man meat."

A little of Ryan's drink dribbled down his chin as he coughed a laugh. "She's a mess."

I rolled my eyes and nodded. "Thank you, Captain Obvious. I did look Decadence up online. It's basically a gay Mardi Gras. Street parties, private parties, alcohol flowing in the streets, beads flying faster than gay slurs, that sort of thing. It looked like a menu of deliciously debauched activities. We can choose to participate in some—or none."

"Huh. Okay. See anything you want to do?"

"Oh yeah. We can't come to New Orleans and skip the street parties. We both need to hobble back to the house with hundreds of beads weighing us down."

He chuckled. "Okay. What else?"

"I've never been to New Orleans. I'd love to do some touristy stuff, maybe while the boys are sleeping off—or on—whatever they do in the wee hours." I thought a moment. "They have these graveyard tours. They sound spooky scary—and a lot of fun. Oh, and everyone says the food there is the best in the world. We have to find some places where locals eat, outside the Quarter. I want to taste *real* New Orleans."

"Was there—"

"Oh, and there's a casino." I turned my whole body toward him, as much as the seat belt would allow. "I *love* casinos, and I'm pretty lucky."

He nodded. "Alright. Casino, check. You mentioned private parties. What did those look like?"

The little devil had been quiet for nearly a year. Something about being in a stable, loving relationship seemed to bore him. His sudden puff of smoke nearly made me drop my drink.

*Michael, Michael, Michael. Are you going to be lame for the rest of your life? You used to be so much fun. Do you remember the silk ties?*

"Hey—"

*Oh, shut up and listen. You're only young once, and with Ryan's body and your ass, you two should be very popular in New Orleans. Promise me you'll go to at least one of the private parties.*

"Fine. Whatever. Can you go away now?" I blew on my shoulder.

Vodka dispels demons. Who knew?

Ryan was staring intently. "You okay?"

"Yeah, sorry, was just thinking through what I found online." He was an understanding guy, but witnessing me chatting with imaginary voices might be a stretch. "So, there's a few parties that look like ads to the bars in Atlanta, straight-up dances. Other than being around new people, I don't think they'd be different from going to any other bar."

"Um, you forget. I've never been to a bar."

My mouth opened but nothing came out. I'd forgotten he was a newborn gay on many levels. It felt really weird to be the guy with experience. Did that make me his daddy? Shit. I was twelve years younger than Ryan. I *couldn't* be his daddy, could I? What were the gay rules on this? I'd definitely have to check the manual when we landed.

"Oh, babe. Okay. We can keep one of those on the list. My little virgin." I caressed his cheek.

"Oh, fuck off. What else?" He couldn't keep the wide smile away.

"There was a party for every flavor. The bears were popular with several nights. Leather and bondage found their way into almost every event. There were a couple bareback parties. The pictures in the ads were pretty clear on what would happen there. Let's see. There were parties every night at every bar, but they sounded like normal bar nights with a promo.

There's a foam party one night. No idea what that means. There weren't any pictures, just an ad full of bubbles and words. One of the big paddle boats is hosting a dinner cruise with a show, probably cheesy musical theater in honor of the gay hoard visiting town."

"Sheesh. This sounds crazy. We've only got three days."

"That's not even half of it. When we get to the hotel, we should see if there are programs or a local newspaper or magazine, like *David* back home. We can pick from the menu easier if it's sitting in front of us."

"Makes sense. At least we won't get bored."

I chuckled. "With Fin and Rob around, you think that's even possible?"

His glass shot into the air for another salute. "Throw in Abe, and we're playing out of our league."

I clinked his glass, then lowered my voice. "I'm a little nervous."

"Aww, babe, it'll be okay. I won't let the big bad bears get ya—unless…"

I smacked his shoulder and laughed. "I have all the wild animals I can handle sitting next to me. Something tells me I might even be out of my depth with him."

He gave me a lecherous grin and Groucho Marx-ed his eyebrows. "I am a Scorpio. Fear my tail."

"I'd rather tap it."

"Promises, promises."

———

WE LANDED IN NEW ORLEANS AND WERE DRIVEN TO our rented home in the heart of heathen heaven. Pride flags flapped nearly everywhere we looked: on poles in front of public buildings, beneath the American flag at McDonald's, even draped above the entrance to the massive casino. It was as if some gay Tinkerbell had sprinkled fairy dust all over the city.

Wait, Tinkerbell was inherently gay, right? Or was that just Peter?

Anyway.

More abundant than the flags were the fags.

Sweet Mother of All Things Gay and Good. They were everywhere.

As we approached Bourbon Street, the driver craned his head and said, "We'll have to go several blocks around Bourbon. The main street is blocked off, but even side streets nearby are clogged. Can't remember a Decadence this big before."

Ryan grinned and gave me a wink.

We got to the house and unpacked. At the airport,

Ryan had grabbed a copy of a newspaper-looking circular called *Southern Decadence Deep Dive*. It was the official order of events and advertisements for the weekend's festivities. By the time I strode into the bedroom, he had it fully splayed across the bed.

"The boys won't get here until late tonight. Why don't we do non-gay things on our first day, then let the guys guide us the rest of the way?"

"Sounds good," I said. "We have a few hours until dinner time. Should we do a little exploring? Maybe do something touristy?"

He folded up the paper and stood. "Whatever you like, babe." He gripped my shoulders and kissed me.

I melted. God, I loved this man.

His hands shifted to my back and he gently guided me down onto the bed, our lips never parting.

An hour later, I finished washing Ryan's sweat off my body and we walked out the door. The sun was beginning to set, but New Orleans still shone brightly. I had no idea it would continue all night. During festival weeks, New Orleans never dimmed.

We took a cab around the mass of partygoers to a quieter section of town where there were shops and restaurants. It was Labor Day weekend, and the Big Easy was a sweltering pot of heat and humidity. I'd thrown on a royal blue tank top and shorts, while Ryan wore my favorite outfit he owned: that stringy, flimsy neon yellow tank top he wore on our second date, the day I fell in love with him. That shirt barely covered his chest, and any decent wind let at least one nipple escape. He caught me staring and shoved me playfully.

"No peeking. We're in public," he teased, then reached down and grabbed my hand.

I couldn't stop myself from gaping down at our clasped palms. When I looked up, he gave me a squeeze and smiled, then turned and pulled me down the street.

For the first time in my life, I walked hand-in-hand with *another man* in public. As gay-friendly as Atlanta was, it was our home. Our coworkers lived there. Our lives were there. Neither of us had been brave enough.

I know, it sounds silly. We weren't scaling a mountain or fighting a war. It was just holding hands, but something about it was terrifying. It simply wasn't done. Society wasn't there yet. *We* weren't there yet.

That day, that beautiful day, we found our way there.

My heart filled and raced—and those are *very* hard things for a heart to do at the same time. I fought back the annoying watering in one eye. Ryan stilled my sappiness with a snicker and snarky grin. That earned him a punch in the shoulder, but I immediately regripped his hand after delivering his well-deserved punishment.

Antique stores outnumbered shops filled with tourist merchandise, and Ryan was giddy. He loved anything old, especially pieces with interesting histories. Most of the shops aimed at tourists displayed T-shirts with humorous sayings plastered across the chest. We bought a matching pair with *Thing 1* and *Thing 2* on them, a reference from the holy works of Dr. Seuss.

As we passed another shop with shirts, Ryan giggled and left me on the sidewalk with instructions to stay where I was. He returned a moment later with a bag in one hand and his poochy, snarky grin stretched across his face. He giggled like a three-year-old as he unfurled a neon yellow tank top with stringy shoulders and script that read, *Don't Make Me Go All Cajun On Your Ass!* He held it over my favorite shirt he was wearing, confirming their color and cut were nearly identical.

The little shit. I loved it.

A voodoo shop caught Ryan's eye and he dragged me across the street like a kid hauling his parent downstairs on Christmas morning. We entered to the jingle of a tiny golden bell attached to the top of the door, and a woman with straggly black hair that fell below her bottom greeted us. Her eyelashes were black. Her lips were black. She'd even outlined the edges of her ears black. She was one creepy fucker.

The tinkling bell was a merry contrast to the eerie sternness of the shopkeeper. "You." Without hesitation, she pointed directly at Ryan. "Come here, boy."

Ryan squeezed my hand then stepped forward. He moved so slowly, walked so stiffly, in a way I hadn't seen all night. The woman's eyes widened as he came closer. I was a little freaked out.

Dozens of intertwined metal and bone necklaces and bangles hanging around the woman's neck clanged as she took two overly dramatic strides forward. Her bony palm flew out to land in the center of Ryan's chest. His body convulsed at her touch. It looked like he'd gone limp and only her hand was keeping him from falling over.

My skin tingled, but I dared not move.

"Your heart is strong. Your will is stronger. You have much, yet you seek still. You yearn. Your yearning will undo you. It will undo you." Her last words rasped out like the hissing of a snake who'd smoked too much.

She yanked her hand away as if his touch burned her, then leaped back a step. Ryan sucked in a breath and regained control of his limbs. I stepped forward and placed a comforting hand on his shoulder.

The woman's head snapped to me and her black-framed gaze locked onto my eyes. I couldn't suppress a shiver. It felt like she was looking inside me; *through* me somehow.

She never spoke, simply shook her head once and lowered her eyes. In a blink, she'd disappeared beyond our view to some back room where black mascara must've been stored in bulk.

*Holy shit*. Ryan was *shaking*.

When he turned and looked at me, his eyes were, I don't know, distant.

We left and continued our stroll in silence. We passed four shops before he clutched my hand again, his palm and fingers slick with sweat, his pulse still racing. Where before his grasp was full of affection and pride, now it felt more like the desperate act of a drowning man. The Jaws of Life couldn't have pried us apart in that moment.

After another ten minutes of silent searching, neither of us really sure what there was to search for, we passed a restaurant with outdoor seating and industrial-size fans to keep diners from melting in the heat. It emanated the smell of sausage and seafood mingled with spices, which nearly made my eyes water—in the best way possible. Without speaking or looking at each other, we veered off the sidewalk and through the ancient door. What little paint was still clinging to its wood was green, I think. La Boucherie, faintly visible, had been painted in elegant script. That paint might've originally been white or yellow. After an eternity under the New Orleans sun, it was invisible ink given a drop of moisture.

As we entered, there were no tablecloths covering rickety wooden tops. No maître d' greeted us, and no white-festooned servers scraped or bowed. One lonely woman who looked older than the door waved from across the dim dining room. She wiped her hands carelessly on her apron that was splattered with tomato sauce and whatever else might've been on the menu as she motioned us forward, sparing herself the extra steps to greet us in the doorway.

Our hands were still clasped.

"Come in, boys. Don't be shy." Her Cajun accent was as thick as her wintery hair. She eyed me up and down, then inspected Ryan, her eyes lingering on our clasped hands.

I self-consciously pulled mine free.

Her bony fingers shot forward faster than I'd thought possible, gripping my wrist, pushing us back together.

"None o' that nonsense, boy. It's clear you two belong together. Don't be 'shamed of it."

My head lowered, embarrassed by her reprimand, then ashamed by my own lack of courage. Staring at my feet, I obeyed, entwining my fingers with Ryan's.

"There. Better. Now, pick a table. Nobody here 'til dark, so ya sit anywhere ya like."

We sat. Ryan reached across the table's rough surface and pulled my hands into his again. That voodoo lady must've really shaken him. When he looked into my eyes, there was something there, something odd, but I never had the chance to explore it—the woman returned from the kitchen with a basket of bread and two glasses of water.

She paused a few feet from our table and sighed loudly.

"Cup 'n' saucer, I swear." There was more warmth in her voice than in the spices I'd smelled earlier. A crooked, toothy smile lit her face. I swear she was the most beautiful woman in the world in that frozen instant.

Ryan's smile finally returned, and his eyes breathed life once more.

I squeezed his hands and suppressed…something.

Ma (that's what she insisted we call her) refused to bring us a menu. Instead, she brought us one course after another. By the end of the night, there were platters of food on neighboring tables and we were ready to waddle back onto the streets. Ryan pulled out his wallet, but Ma materialized and the same claw that had seized my wrist descended on his.

"Oh no. Ya don't get t' leave without eatin' my

special bread puddin'. Best in town. Ever'body say so."

Ryan started to object, but she waved him off and vanished into the kitchen. I was chuckling when he turned back to me. All I could do was shrug and grin. There was no refusing Ma anything, that was clear by now.

And there was no denying her unmatched skill in the kitchen either.

The bread pudding was more than a dessert. It was an experience.

No, it was a *sexual* experience.

I might've had a pudding-gasm right there at the table as Ryan's eyes rolled in the back of his head. It had been years since I'd eaten that much, but we weren't about to leave a crumb of that bread pudding or a drop of its criminally delicious, sticky-sweet, cherry vanilla caramel bourbon sauce in the bowl. Ma caught Ryan using a finger to dig the last of it out. She cackled and hugged him. When he leaned into her ample bosom, she squeezed him tight and kissed the top of his head.

"Ya make t's old woman swoon, young 'un."

Ryan smiled up. "This has been the best first night in New Orleans we could've hoped for. Thank you, Ma. Could you bring our check? We'd better walk some of this off before it gets too late."

"Pshaw." She waved her hand again. "Twenty bucks should do it."

"Twenty dollars?" Ryan's wallet dropped to the table. "That bread pudding alone was worth twenty bucks!"

"And seein' you two look at each other like ya do was worth a hell of a lot more. Now, give me that twenty and get outta here." She held out a palm and playfully smacked the back of Ryan's head. There was no arguing with this woman.

He dug out a twenty and handed it to her. "Can I at least tip my server? She was amazing."

Ma barked a laugh and blushed. "Young 'un, you's a mess. Do what ya like."

It took her a minute to stop laughing, then she wheeled toward me and stabbed a crooked finger in the air. "And don't *you* be lettin' go o' him again, ya hear?"

"Yes, ma'am." I grinned and grabbed Ryan's free hand.

Ma's smile somehow widened, and she clutched her hands to her chest, then tottered away. Ryan pulled out two Benjamins and hid them under the dessert bowl.

"Mr. Big Tipper," I teased.

"Her food was amazing. Her service was amazing. Even her advice was amazing."

"Her advice?" I asked.

"Yeah. She told you not to let go of me again. She's a wise woman."

I laughed and tossed my napkin at him as we stood to leave.

He grabbed my hand and raised it to his lips as we ventured back into the New Orleans heat.

4

———

## THE FOAM FAIRY

We hadn't planned on doing anything decadent that night. We were determined to enjoy the city, its food and culture, without the clamor of dance music and pulsating bodies—at least for one night. But, as we walked back to the main road to hail a cab, Ryan turned to me with a glimmer in his eye.

"Uh-oh. I know that look," I said with a grin.

He usually held himself with confidence, near cockiness. In that moment, he gave me the most sheepish look I think I'd ever seen cross his face.

*You know that means you're screwed, right?* The little angel's voice whispered in my head. My bicameral conscience hadn't spoken to me in months, maybe a year. For some reason, it was a welcome sound that made me grin.

*Wipe that goofy grin off your face and agree to*

*whatever he's about to say. I like the look in his eyes. He's definitely up to something, and I bet it's naughty.* The devil materialized on my shoulder, wearing the same green-and-gold outfit the marshal of last year's Mardi Gras parade had worn, complete with a tall, feathery top hat. He spun his cane and shook the tails on his long coat.

Now I was nervous. Those two wouldn't show up for any random recreation.

"So," Ryan continued. "There's this event you mentioned a while back, when we were deciding whether or not to come on this trip. It sounded, um, intriguing, something I've never done, and it's only happening once during Decadence."

"Okay. I'm listening."

"The foam party."

"Foam party?"

He stopped walking and faced me. "Yeah. I'm not completely sure what it is. I think it's like a pool party, but instead of wading in water, you're submerged in bubbles of some kind. Don't ask me why I'm so curious about it. I just am."

Before my counselors could chime in, I grinned and nodded. "If my baby is curious, we have to check it out. Do we need to go back to the house for anything?"

His grin widened. "Nope. The paper said they have lockers for our clothes."

My brows shot up. "Our clothes? *All* our clothes?"

His grin turned downright lecherous. "Yep. Every last piece. You don't get to wear anything, mister, only bubbles."

The angel gasped. The devil cackled. I smiled weakly, nodded, and followed Ryan toward a waiting cab.

———

A QUICK CAB RIDE LATER, WE WALKED INTO A LARGE warehouse. The event organizers had installed tall screens and lockers, creating two dressing rooms to either side of a large, open expanse. The entrance was fully walled off from the main area, so we still had no idea what we were getting into as we paid the fee and accepted a folded towel from the doorman.

The familiar heartbeat of dance music vibrated through my chest as we entered one of the dressing rooms. A few other guys were disrobing, wrapping towels around their waists and locking their belongings in metal lockers. I noticed most of them still wearing underwear beneath their terrycloth wrap. Ryan rolled his eyes, reading my mind, and stepped out of his underwear. Everyone in the room stilled and stared. He was glorious—and nearly hard.

*Holy shit.* When had that happened?

He motioned for me to follow suit, so I self-consciously slipped out of my undies and donned my towel.

"Tsk, tsk, tsk," Ryan hissed in my ear as one hand reached around from behind and rubbed my cock through the towel. His teeth and tongue teased my earlobe. "This is *my* fantasy, remember. My rules. That towel goes in a locker."

I looked down and his hard-on twitched.

Sexy, sneaky, *bossy* bastard.

But who was I to argue?

My towel flew across the room into a locker, quickly followed by the rest of my clothes.

I'm not sure either of us were prepared for what we saw as we rounded the corner onto the main floor. A sea of bubbles, a veritable ocean, spanned the full length of the warehouse and rose to our chests. A couple hundred guys stood around the perimeter, only their heads and shoulders fully visible. Most were chatting and laughing in small groups. A few brave souls danced in the center of the room.

Ryan, ever fond of a stage, grabbed my hand and dragged me to the heart of the bubble bazaar, where everyone in the place could see us. At this point, our nakedness was masked as much as everyone else's. They had no idea Ryan was fully erect, or that he was pulling me forward by my dick rather than my hand, stroking me as we waded through suds. If they had been closer, maybe they would've recognized the shivering of my shoulders or the faraway look in my eyes each time his fingers ran the length of me, but they were a good twenty yards away.

The moment we reached the room's center, Ryan turned, wrapped his arms around me, and pressed his hard, muscled body against mine. Soapy goodness squished between us, and my dick leapt to full attention.

We held each other close, swaying to the music, our bodies slipping and sliding, our abs grinding. I could feel his pulse through his dick. It raced. It pounded. Every time it twitched, my body spasmed and my own twitch sent lightning down my spine. I remembered where we were and glanced around. Everyone else had left the dance floor and were staring from the safety of the sideline. Some gaped with intrigue, others grinned, a few whispered and pointed. Before I could whisper a protest, Ryan gripped my head with both hands and pulled my face into his, into a deep, passionate kiss.

The staring men vanished. The warehouse disappeared. Only Ryan and his mouth and tongue remained.

Oh, and his throbbing cock.

We kissed through the next song, and the next. By the third song, Ryan's hands had fallen from my head and were rubbing and caressing my shoulders and back. My fingers traced the outline of his chest, then teased the ends of his nipples. I felt his body quake at my touch, and my world spun. Then my body spun as he turned me away from him and pressed his hardened cock between my cheeks, grinding it up and down, brushing my hole each time it passed. My head fell backward to rest on his shoulder and his hand wrapped around and gripped my chest. He ground in time with the music.

George Michael's voice boomed through the speakers, and one of our favorite old-school anthems rang out. Cheers rose from around the room, and guys sang along, yet none ventured onto the floor—onto *our* floor.

The first chorus began, and hundreds of voices cried, "Freedom," as Ryan finally slid inside me. He used his hands to pull my body against his, forcing his full length into me. The bubbles or suds or floaty lube —whatever that stuff was—worked to perfection, and he slid effortlessly in and out. My back arched. I couldn't open my eyes. I wanted him to live inside me forever, to never pull out, to find a way to plant his whole being in my soul.

The singing stopped as someone noticed Ryan obviously fucking me beneath the bubble sea. I heard the murmur of the crowd, but didn't care. Let them watch. The thrill of being watched added to the thousand other sensations, nearly overwhelming my mind. Ryan's hand reached down to stroke me, but I pushed it away. I didn't want this to end.

Two songs later, Ryan was thrusting slowly, then holding me without moving. I felt his pulse inside me, and thrilled at the idea of his heart beating within my body. We didn't move. We couldn't move. Then I felt his lips kiss my ear and he said, "I love you so much."

I reached back with my hands and gripped his head, twining my fingers in his hair. He kissed my neck, then turned my head to kiss me awkwardly. His hips pressed again. Slowly. Softly. Then a beat faster. Then harder. By the time George Michael was a distant memory, Ryan was pressing himself into me with hunger and need. His body tensed, and I knew he was getting close. When his hand reached down a second time, I gladly gave myself to his touch. He stroked and thrusted; we both ached for release. Seconds later, I felt him fill me and I spilled across his hand and into the sudsy sea. I swore he'd been saving up because that was the most I'd ever felt from him—and I loved it. It felt like the most I'd ever shot too.

When his thrusting stilled, we resumed our swaying to the music, him inside me, for another two songs. I finally opened my eyes and caught one group of a dozen guys clapping politely, fingers into palms. They giggled and grinned appreciatively. Ryan just growled into my ear and licked it.

*Holy shit.* He was getting hard again.

At that moment, the event organizers decided to enforce the No Sex on the Dance Floor sign we'd clearly missed. Our faithful fans groaned as a staffer motioned for us to move off the floor. We giggled when the staffer winced as Ryan pulled out and I shivered.

Served him right.

Who knew we loved bubbles so much?

---

THE DAY PASSED IN A BLUR. FIN, ROB, AND ABE WERE determined to visit every gay bar in the city, even creating a list they checked off as we hit each one. We started midday Saturday on the main strip. Fin had accidentally trashed the page with parade details, so we weren't sure if the main event was to be held on Saturday or Sunday. Either way, we wanted to see

the show, so we strolled one block to check
things out.

Bourbon Street was packed. Thousands of men
and women—who am I kidding, they were almost all
men—flooded the party district. I'm not sure why that
surprised me, but we could barely squirm our way
through the throng of thongs, and more streamed in
from side streets every minute.

As with Decadence's straight cousin, Mardi Gras,
music blasted from speakers hung from balconies
where the privileged few gawked, waved, and tossed
beaded necklaces. Newcomers flashed their tits in
exchange for beaded necklaces, but quickly learned
the stakes for prizes at Decadence were significantly
higher than at Fat Tuesday. Most were already sweaty
and shirtless, so the better necklaces were only earned
by a quick drop of a dude's undies—and a remarkable
number of men were *only* wearing undies or Speedos.

Yes, sports fans, we saw flesh flash faster than
wieners at a dog show.

In addition to the mostly naked men waving their,
um, pride, others in flashy and flamboyant feathery
outfits danced and paraded about. The costumed
wonders mostly floated on the outer edges of the
crowd to avoid crushing their precious wearable art.
Ryan pointed at one particularly crazy outfit, then I
directed him to a hedonistic hottie who was simulating

a sex act with his bodybuilder buddy. We laughed as our heads snapped about in a constant blur of sensual sensory overload.

It was people-watcher heaven, and we weren't going to miss a single thing, even if our neck muscles hated us the next morning.

When the heat of the sun and sweat became too much, Fin or Rob would motion to the next bar on the magical list, and our conga line of friends snaked our way to its entrance. I'd been to a number of gay bars in Nashville and Atlanta, but there were few places that competed with the outright opulence of New Orleans.

As we entered the first bar, a three-story joint on the corner of Bourbon and they-sell-alcohol street, my eyes darted up toward a flash of motion—or should I say a *flesh* of motion? Go-go dancers in Atlanta were common, but they wore swim trunks or thongs that covered their things. The law—and Southern sensibilities—demanded it.

But holy shit, Dorothy, we weren't in Atlanta anymore.

The dancer above me wore a *sock* zip-tied over his snake—and it was a freakin' barracuda. The sock was one of those knee-high kinds I wore in high school gym class.

*Dude, respect the stocking!* the little devil's voice cackled in my head.

The snake's eggs dangled and flopped freely as he danced. His ass was completely exposed—unless you counted the dollar bill athletically clutched between his cheeks as cover. I'd never seen such a public display of nudity—well, unless you counted the dedicated bead-earners in the street, but they weren't on-the-clock working stiffs (excuse the pun).

Ryan punched my shoulder to wake me out of my ball-induced trance. His eyes danced with mischief and mirth as he grabbed my hand and pulled me through to where the others stood, drinks already in hand. Abe handed us bright yellow twisty plastic cups. The necks were thin and stretched a good foot or more long, I guessed simulating a hurricane's funnel. Inside was the most devilishly delicious fruit-punch concoction I had ever tasted.

Ryan beamed as he watched me take my first sip. My eyes bugged out a bit before settling on his. Damn, it had a lot of alcohol—but I knew showing weakness meant death in this jungle, so I took another long pull and resisted a visible wince with every fiber of my being. By the third sip, I couldn't feel my lips, and I wasn't sure my body was capable of wincing anymore.

Fucking Ryan laughed and clanked his plastic against mine.

Why did I love the bastard so much? Please explain that to me.

---

As the sun finally began to set, hunger overcame drunkenness. Our little gaggle wandered two blocks off the main drag to a restaurant Rob had found on their initial drive from the airport. It was one of those places decorated in gaudy green-and-gold drapes with equally colorful masks glaring down from the walls. The wait staff all wore Mardi Gras themed camouflage, swirling patterns of black, green, and gold. The place reeked of tourists, but we were too drunk to care. Ryan had mediocre jambalaya, while I ate an equally adequate steak with bourbon sauce.

"So," Rob started before draining half his glass of water in a weak attempt to stave off a headache. "There's this party tonight."

Ryan perked up. "Yeah? What kind tonight? We found one last night." He gave me a sneaky sidelong grin with one raised brow.

"Oh sweet Jesus. Did you two find a prayer service before your weekend of wildness?" Fin teased.

"Something like that. Michael did call out for God a few times, if that counts," Ryan said seriously.

I turned forty shades of red, covered my face with a palm, and heard Ryan bark out a laugh.

"Lord, we don't need to hear about your marital bliss, Dad. Let us kids have our innocence a little longer," Rob said.

Ryan dribbled wine as he laughed. "Innocent? You three? You're the most corrupting influence in our lives, thank you very much."

"And you love us for it, dear." Fin leaned across and patted Ryan's hand with his meaty palm.

We all laughed and raised our glasses in salute.

Ryan's hand found my leg under the table and squeezed affectionately. The shiver the hurricane had numbed returned and I felt warmth trickle through my chest.

"Here are your choices tonight, people. One: the street party on Bourbon. It's more of what we did today, but with a bigger crowd, more beads, far less clothing, and a stage with live bands. The other option is a place called Rough Riders."

"Rough Riders? Is that a country bar?" I asked.

Rob laughed. "Not exactly. It's a sex club."

I remember dropping my fork, but little else.

Ryan's grip on my leg tightened.

"Sex club?" Ryan asked. I wasn't sure if his tone

held more confusion, aversion, or intrigue—probably a little of each.

Fin flexed a bicep. "You'll get to see more of this in action. Hell, you might even *get* some action. I've been there before, but never during Decadence. It's going to be wild."

Ryan looked to me, but I sat frozen. My mind couldn't process the idea of watching other men surrounding him, naked with him, or—no, I couldn't even think that. I looked down at my plate.

"I think we'll do the street party with the bands," Ryan said, much quicker and with more steel in his voice than I expected. I looked up and he was watching me. He rubbed my leg gently and offered a tight smile.

He knew what I was thinking. The sex-starved Scorpio in him wanted to find out more about Rough Riders. Hell, a part of me was curious. But if we went there, other guys would want to touch Ryan, to do more than just touch him. God, I hated always being that guy, the wet blanket on Rob or Fin's wild ideas. I wasn't ashamed of only wanting a life with Ryan, of not wanting to share him, but they sometimes made me feel small for having such simple, old-fashioned dreams.

This time, I didn't have to object or look like the prude at the table. Ryan protected me.

*That's* why I loved the bastard so much.

My hand found his.

Abe, our most festive friend, stepped in. "I think that sounds perfect. There will probably be more passed around than men at that sex party. We'll see more dick on the street anyway. Yay, dick for everybody!"

And yes, I loved Abe too, the fruity fucker.

I thought I caught a slight evil-eye from Rob, but it vanished as quickly as it had appeared. Fin looked disappointed, but didn't say anything.

After dinner, we returned to the house to shower and change. Ryan donned tight blue jeans and an even tighter-fitting white Ruel shirt. His arms bulged out of the bands meant to contain far less meaty men, and his chest…fuck, how was I supposed to look at his nipples spearing the sheer white fabric of his shirt all night and not want to lick or bite them?

He caught me staring. "Like it?"

"Damn, babe. You're killin' me and we haven't even left the house yet."

He grinned and traced his index finger around a nipple. "Is this what you want? You like these old things?"

I couldn't take it anymore, and shoved him back onto the bed. My hands flew up under his shirt and gripped his chest like I was juicing oranges. When my body pressed against his, I felt his arousal—and he could feel my excitement just as much.

"Now, now," he said, gently lifting me off him. "Don't get me all wrinkled before we go out. What would the boys think?"

"They'd think you needed to take that damn shirt off, same as what I'm thinking right now."

He growled and nipped at my neck. "Later. I'm going to make you beg when we get back."

"Please? Really? I'll start begging now if it'll help."

He laughed and tossed me onto the bed where he'd just been. "You're hopeless. Get dressed. The guys want to leave soon."

I jumped into my favorite come-fuck-me jeans. It took several minutes of wriggling and bouncing to get them over my hips and fastened, but they looked like a fantastic outer layer of blue skin when I was finished. They gripped my ass so tight my crack was visible. Ryan was gonna die. He hadn't seen me wear those jeans since our first few months together, back when I was still trying to win him with my, um, more impressive qualities.

When I strode into the den, he eyed me up and down like I was on the menu of the restaurant we'd left an hour before. He hopped off the couch and ran his hands over my quads, then reached around and played my ass like a piano.

"Fuck. I can't even make an impression. When did your ass turn into stone?" He poked at a cheek with two fingers.

"Stick with me, old man. You might get some of that later if you're good." I leaned in and bit his poochy lower lip.

"Oh shit. Now you're not playing fair."

"Nope. And I never will. Deal with it." I grinned up at him and was rewarded with a broad smile of his own.

"You two are going to make me puke, and I just changed into clean clothes." Rob made a gagging sound. Fin, never one to be left out, joined in the mock vomit.

Abe sighed loudly. "I could watch them all night."

"Ha. I knew you were one of those perverts who liked to watch!" Rob said.

"If we'd known you liked to watch, you should've joined us for the foam party on Friday night," Ryan said.

"Hey—" I gave Ryan a wide-eyed glance.

"Foam party? And just what were you doing in this foam our dear little Abe would want to watch?"

"Enough to get kicked out before we could start a

second round." Ryan stroked my cheek with mock sincerity.

He loved watching me squirm sometimes, and he knew this subject was doing it. We might've had sex in front of hundreds of dudes, but there were layers of foam protecting our pride. Here, there was nothing between us and the judgment of jurors one and two.

Abe scooted to the edge of the couch and leaned forward. "We really need to hear details."

"We need to get going. I heard some guys talking earlier. There's a surprise guest singer coming, and some thought it might be Deborah Cox. We can't miss her," Fin said.

"Deborah Cox? As in, 'Mr. Lonely' Deborah Cox?" I asked.

"Hey, choir boy knows his anthem queens," Rob snarked.

"Ha ha. Very funny. I know how to shake my booty as much as the next bad-dancing white guy." I turned to Ryan. "We can't miss Deborah Cox. I might die."

He snorted. "Alright. You heard him. We have a life-and-death dance situation here. Move, people."

And so we moved.

Deborah Cox indeed graced us with her royal presence. She was the queen of the gay dance stage and didn't disappoint. After two songs, she started to leave and the crowd erupted. She gave in and sang another three songs. By the time she started 'Absolutely Not,' we were screaming at the top of our lungs. Thousands of hands flew into the air and a sea of half-naked men hopped in time with the heavy bass.

Abe, never to be out-queened, even by the indomitable Ms. Cox, drag-synced every word, his index finger flying in accusation and sass the whole time. Each time the lyrics hit the words "Absolutely not," he put a palm into Ryan's chest and pushed him back against the crowd behind us. They were annoyed the first time, but quickly caught on and swayed back to let him fall before catching and pushing him back up. Before I knew what had happened, Abe had dozens around us wrapped into his act.

And our dear Deborah led thousands as they screamed "Absolutely not!" into the steamy New Orleans night.

***

ROB AND FIN VANISHED INTO THE CROWD AFTER Deborah left the stage. Abe hopped to look over the heads of the much taller men around us, but was not able to see where they'd gone. He turned back to us and yelled over the music, "What are you guys doing now?"

Ryan, without even looking at me, shouted back, "I promised Michael something. We're going to head out soon."

My brows rose. He smirked and winked, then mouthed, "Beg for it."

I missed a step in our dance and nearly knocked us all over.

Abe steadied us and shouted, "I can't compete with whatever that was. You kids have fun. I'm going to stay here and find a boy to ravage. If I'm not back by Christmas, send the National Guard."

We laughed and watched as Abe wiggled his way through to a pack of shirtless, sweaty men who had clearly taken more than aspirin to enhance their evening of entertainment.

Ryan grabbed me around the waist and pulled me into him, pressing a deep kiss to my lips. When his mouth opened and his tongue pried into mine, I felt all of New Orleans light up with fireworks. Before I knew what he was doing, my shirt was flying off over my head to the applause and cheers of those around us. I opened my eyes to catch him doing that crossed-arms shirt-pull thing models did on TV. Damn, it was a hot move. The guys who'd cheered for my striptease erupted in squeals and hoots for Ryan's Adonis-like physique. He was hard and sweaty. In the lamplight of the street, his chest and abs glistened. I nearly jizzed my jeans.

Thank everything holy they were too tight to allow blood flow—or any other kind of flow.

He tucked our shirts into a belt loop, then held me tight against him as we danced. The heat of his body, combined with the constant slipping and sliding of our sweaty skin, made me harder than the street we danced on. His erection kept bumping mine through our jeans, sending jolts through my soul.

And the fucker saw it. It was in his eyes. He knew exactly what he was doing, and he redoubled his efforts, grinding into me, dragging his hardened nipples against mine, licking the sweat off my neck before devouring the tender skin above my collarbone.

Hands reached out from every direction, teasing and touching, rubbing us, pressing us together. Ryan's mouth enveloped mine, and he didn't allow me a breath to look up and see who was touching us. Two, then three, then more men surrounded us, their hands no longer gentle, rubbing and stroking my back and neck, some drifting to feel the tautness of my ass in its painted-on jeans. Then bodies pressed into my sides and back. They must've done the same to Ryan because he squeezed tighter against me. My pulse raced with excitement and a hint of terror, but just as I began to feel walls closing in, Ryan's hot breath blew into my ear.

"You want to get out of here?"

"Yes, please."

"Told ya you'd beg."

"Fuck you, asshole." He squeezed my dick through my jeans and I moaned. "Take me out of here *now*. I want you inside me all night."

"That's my boy."

<hr>

IT WAS NOON ON SUNDAY BEFORE THE ENTIRE CLAN rose from their slumber.

After Deborah Cox's inspired performance, Rob and Fin had slipped the crowd and attended their sex party. Fin, a monster of a man who rarely lost control —and was supposedly a total top—was walking bowlegged and looked like there wasn't enough coffee in the city to rouse his bleary brain. He winced slightly as he sat at the table.

"Uh, Fin, did you let a city bus park up your ass last night?" I teased.

"Shut the fuck up. Why are you yelling? Why is everybody yelling? And why is my ass raw?"

"Oh, honey, it's not nearly as raw as it was last night." Rob glided into the room as if he'd gotten a full ten hours of rest. "I saw at least four men fuck you on that Ping-Pong table. I got distracted and missed how your game of pool went."

"There was this cue—"

"And I'm officially too young to hear any of this," I cut him off, then winked at Rob.

"Oh no, dear, you're exactly the right age to learn from your Aunty Fin."

"Aunty?" Fin protested.

"Nobody who gets gang-fucked like you did last night gets to be the uncle. Just deal with it, sweetness."

For once, Ryan couldn't think of anything to say. I was staring, mouth open again, unsure whether to look at Rob or Fin.

"So, basically, you guys either fucked or got fucked all night? By a bunch of random strangers in a bar?" Abe asked.

Rob grinned and nodded. "Yep. It was fabulous. Hottest orgy I've seen in years—and I've been around, honey."

"Oh, we know," Abe said.

"Shh. Respect those with more experience."

"I'm not sure respect is what you get when you let a football team of strangers pound you all night," I said.

"Oh, Michael, it's exactly what you get. Oh, and

the skanky-ho test regime at the doctor. That's a necessity too."

Ryan shook his head and laughed.

"So," Abe said, looking between Ryan and me over his coffee. "What did you two love birds do last night? You were getting pretty steamy when I left you."

"Oh, we danced a while longer and came back here, got a good night's sleep. You know us, just an old married couple." Ryan nudged my knee with his under the table.

In reality, we *had* come back to the house after a few more songs, but I doubted we got any more sleep than Rob and Fin. Ryan hadn't been kidding when he said he wanted to do an all-nighter. Foreplay lasted so long I thought I was going to explode. Every time he got me close, he'd slap my hand and pin my wrists above my head, careful to keep his body from even touching mine.

"All night means *all night*, mister," he said, over and over. His voice was rough and low, almost a growl. The sound of it nearly made me come—but I resisted. If he wanted an all-nighter, I was darn sure going to try.

In the end, we fell asleep with him inside me, much like when we'd first met. I still have no idea how he kept himself up there all night, but when I woke to his lips roaming up and down my neck, we were still one person. That's what he liked to call it.

*Fuck. One person.* This guy was destroying me.

In what world did anyone deserve that much happiness? How did I deserve it?

I still shiver thinking back on that morning.

"You guys fly out tonight?" Rob's voice shattered my vision of our waking moments.

"Yeah, unfortunately. I wish we'd taken a few extra days off so we could stay longer," Ryan said. I nodded in agreement. New Orleans had been a blast.

Just then, somewhere in the city, a church's bells tolled twice.

"Shit. Two o'clock. We'd better get showered and packed," Ryan said. "Our flight's at six."

And just like that, we said goodbye to our friends and the City of Brotherly Sin…I mean, love…uh, that's a different town.

New Orleans. We said goodbye to New Orleans.

## 5

## THE HUMPBACKED CAT

The holiday season packed a punch in our house. Our two-year anniversary was followed by Thanksgiving, then Ryan's birthday, then Christmas. By the time January rolled around, I was ready to *not* celebrate anything. Who knew merriment could be so exhausting?

And yet, with the winds of winter came that accursed holiday when any self-respecting Irishman wore head-to-toe black and mourned. Yes, I speak of Valentine's Day.

It was a massacre, people, not a day of chocolates and roses. Good people died many years ago—at least, I think they did. I never was good with my Valentine's Day Massacre history. It was just a fun story to tell people when I was single and bitter and would not participate in their stupid ritual.

Fucking Ryan changed all that.

Asshole.

Valentine's Day fell on Saturday. I woke to the smell of eggs and bacon. Fresh coffee followed. Ryan called something in a chipper, cheery voice that would normally get him jailed, but I dragged my ass downstairs anyway. The table was set with white linen and red roses scattered about a centerpiece of brilliant irises. Purple and red might not be the chicest combination to a designer, but for a boy from Tennessee who didn't know his man even knew the state's official flower, I was overwhelmed.

"You, sit." He made a bossy motion with his spatula.

The moment my butt hit wood, coffee was poured. Wave after wave of breakfast foods followed. Ryan must've been at this for hours. I got a little misty sitting there watching him scurry about —*for me*.

"Eat up before it gets cold. I'll be there as soon as these eggs are ready. We have a full day, so don't be shy with your breakfast."

"A full day?" I mumbled through a bite of buttery biscuit.

"Yep, and don't ask, I'm not telling you anything." He sounded very proud of himself. I had no idea why, but in that moment, I knew I was toast. That thought proved prophetic a moment later when Ryan handed me an actual piece of toast.

———

AN HOUR LATER, WE WERE ON THE ROAD. RYAN'S only instructions were to dress comfortably in shorts and tennis shoes—no flip-flops. He said we might be on our feet all day. There was a gleam in his eye I couldn't quite recognize, similar to when a little boy is up to something he thinks is the coolest thing in the world. It was mixed with—I don't know—something *more*. I wasn't sure I'd seen that exact look from him before. An overriding sense of excitement and giddiness wafted off him.

We drove beyond the safety of the Perimeter, known to the gays of Atlanta as the Fruit Loop. I'm sure somewhere there were guys shivering at the thought we'd left the motherland. The houses thinned, replaced by sprawling fields with tightly packed rows of some grain or vegetable. I wasn't a farmer. If it didn't come in a plastic package, how was I to know what it was?

Out of the agricultural nothingness of rural Georgia, a small town square rose. It was as if someone had planted a courthouse, pharmacy, and several storefronts back in the 1800s and they'd only recently sprung from the earth. As we neared, I noticed dozens of shops, mostly antique stores, flowing from the town's center. Beyond the square, side streets flowed in every direction. Old white houses with tall columns and wraparound porches dotted the landscape. It was picturesque, in a lost-in-time and totally-too-far-from-civilization sort of way.

Ryan drove purposefully into the heart of the square and parked in front of one of the antique shops. He reached over, squeezed my hand, then climbed out of the car. I took a deep breath before following. My Spidey sense was tingling its ass off.

A perfectly manicured sign with golden cursive lettering read, The Humpbacked Cat.

*Bing-bong-bing.* The door chime rang as we entered.

The smell of old wood and leather tickled my nose. Everywhere I looked, there were desks and dressers, tables and chairs, mirrors and artwork—and there couldn't have been a single piece younger than one hundred years old. I had died and gone to antique heaven.

I trailed my fingers across a rolltop desk that made my heart quiver. It was cherry and elegant; its placard placed its making around 1700. My hand yanked back, as if a simple touch could damage the work of art before me.

"See anything you like?" Ryan asked from across the shop. He stood next to a long, glass-topped case. A black cat was nuzzling his hand, curling its tail around his arm as he scratched its ear. I walked over to them and saw an odd deformity. The cat was indeed humpbacked.

"Everything here is incredible. I can't get over how new so many old things can look. It's like traveling back in time to when they were made."

He nodded, but didn't look up from the cat.

A moment of silence stretched. I continued gawking at the surrounding antiques, unaware of Ryan's sudden movement. When I turned back, the cat was alone on the case, and Ryan was down on one knee.

I took an involuntary step back.

"Babe." Ryan's voice shook in a way I'd never heard before. "I love you more than anything in the world—except maybe your lasagna." He actually winked. The fucker. "I can't imagine my life without you; without us. Spend the rest of yours with me. Please."

I couldn't believe what I was hearing. My heart was racing so fast I thought it might leap out of my chest. Moisture beaded at the corners of my eyes. My hands were shaking when he took them in his and looked back up. His crystal-gray eyes were so clear, so unwaveringly pure—and they were also filled with moisture.

"Ryan…I…Do you…Are you actually…"

"Please. Just say yes."

"Yes! Oh, God, yes. With all my heart, yes."

He leapt to his feet, wrapped his arms around me, and kissed me with a gentle fervor reserved for the gods of Olympus. The moisture teasing my eyes turned into a salty, messy stream, and we both started giggling at the dribbling mess we were making on the store's floor. I took his face in both my hands and pulled his gaze back to mine, searching for any sign of doubt or fear or, I don't know, something. There was nothing in his gaze but unrelenting love.

I'd thought the last of my protective barriers had fallen some time ago, but that was the moment I became truly vulnerable and exposed. I couldn't hold back. This man whom I loved with all my being— this beautiful, kind, obnoxiously funny man—he wanted me. Forever. *Me.*

Somewhere between amazement, disbelief, and abject joy, I felt my heart unfurl the last of itself to him. It was his completely, without reservation, now and forever.

I was his.

The sound of a nose blowing turned both our heads. Behind the counter, stroking the malformed kitty, was a spindly elderly woman who rose no taller than Ryan's chest. Her wispy gray was dappled with brackish strands. Her horn-rims dated back to the '60s. And yet, the only thing I saw in that moment was her smile. It was brilliant. And she was crying.

No, she was *ugly* crying.

And that made me cry even harder. Then Ryan joined in.

We were a blithering, blubbering mess.

When tears turned back to laughter, it took a long moment for any of us to catch a breath. It was the most beautiful moment I had ever experienced.

"Michael, this is Ruth. She owns this shop." The cat darted from Ruth to Ryan. "And this is Q."

I cocked my head.

"Q, for Quasimodo, the Humpback of Notre Dame."

When my blank stare turned into, well, nothing—it stayed blank—Ryan and Ruth chuckled.

"The original 1939 movie with Charles Laughton is my favorite. I love old movies," Ruth said. "Oh, bugger me, I love anything old."

Her voice was scratchy and warm at the same time, like an old robe whose softness had faded but was still somehow the most comforting wrap in the world.

"Do you know why we're here?" Ryan asked.

I looked around, baffled, then shook my head. "No. I'm all about what just happened, but this isn't where I would've ever expected that. I didn't expect… I mean—"

Ryan laughed again. "We're here to find rings."

My mouth turned into a small O, but wouldn't cooperate with anything more complicated. *What the actual hell?* He'd planned this all out. He wanted to buy rings. This was really happening.

"We can't get married, so I figured the next best thing was to get rings. Screw the state. Let's tell the world we belong to each other."

Well, fucking fuckety fuck. I was crying again.

I'm not a crier. I don't cry. But damn it, I was blubbering.

Ruth darted around the counter faster than I had thought she could move. Before I knew what was happening, her arms held me snugly, and I was being guided to the glass-topped case. Through the watery haze, a sea of silver, gold, and platinum spread before me. I looked up at Ryan. He was grinning from ear to ear. He nodded and motioned for me to peruse the options.

*Holy shit*. This was happening.

I remember Ryan's hand gripping mine as we leaned over the case, examining each ring as though we sought the Holy Grail in a cave full of replicas.

One must not "choose poorly," as the old man had said to Harrison Ford.

After twenty minutes, we hadn't found anything we liked—and liked was not even the standard. We had to freakin' *love* these rings. These were forever rings.

"Oh, honey, I can have something custom made, if ya don't see anything ya like." Ruth stroked my hand almost as much as she did Q. It was oddly soothing.

Ryan tugged at my elbow in the *I want to tell you something private* signal we'd cooked up a year ago.

"Can I look around a bit, then come back to the rings?" I asked Ruth.

Her eyes lit up. "Of course, honey, take all the time ya like. I'll make sure you two get a good deal on anything in the shop." Her calloused fingers patted my cheek before I could escape.

I wandered slowly to the corner where Ryan studied a tall armoire that looked to be colonial or Victorian.

What am I saying? I had no idea. It was old.

He leaned down and whispered, "I have a bunch of other places to visit next. If you don't absolutely love any of those rings, let's keep looking."

I had to kiss him. His cheek was too close not to. He pressed his head against mine and nuzzled me like Q had done to him earlier.

"Let's keep looking."

He nodded, then walked over to the counter. "Ruth, we're going to see the town, maybe get some lunch. We'll be back later."

"I'll be here, Ryan. Won't close this place 'til ya get back."

"Thanks, Ruthie." He leaned over the counter and gave her a peck on the cheek. She giggled and shooed him away with a wave.

When the door clicked shut behind us, I turned toward him. "Ruthie?"

He chuckled. "I've known her for years. She's practically family."

"You little sneak."

He beamed, but just pointed across the square at our next destination. The sign read, McGuinnes Jewelry.

Everything in McGuinnes was sparkly and new, a stark contrast with the historic feel of Ruth's collection. Nothing suited our fancy.

Two shops later, our stomachs were growling. Ryan led me two streets off Main to a house that had been converted into an Irish pub. I had my favorite— shepherd's pie—and Ryan ate bangers and mash.

"Go figure, the big queen chose the giant wiener," I teased after the waiter dropped off our food. Ryan's meal was more appropriately titled Banger and Mash, as there was only one sausage. It was long, thick, and covered the length of his platter-style plate. One end of the meaty schlong rested on a bed of mashed potatoes. Because of the way the chef had laid the sausage, the potatoes looked more anatomical than gastronomical. I made pained groans every time he cut into his meat.

"Don't be jealous of my meat. I can't help it if I bang with the best o' them." His Irish accent was terrible, coming out more drunk Chinese than Irish.

"Can't argue with you there. You are a top banger."

He saluted with a piece of sausage stuck to his fork.

After lunch, we hit three more stores, but didn't find anything to match our marital mood. As if the feline fates guided our steps, we found ourselves back at the door to Ruth's Humpbacked Cat. Ryan raised a questioning brow, and I shrugged, opening the door to be greeted by a loud meow.

"I knew ya'd be back. This day's too special to go anywhere else." Ruth hooked a hand through each of our arms and escorted us toward the counter. "I expect we'll be making rings for you two, but take another look at the case anyway. Ya never know."

We did, and quickly realized she'd been right about the custom job.

"How does this work?" Ryan asked. "I've never had a ring made before, especially one this important."

My heart thrilled just hearing him say things like that. He wasn't cold by any means, but he tended toward the reserved side of expression. For Ryan Alan Lowell to speak so openly and with such affection…I barely knew how to breathe.

I really was toast.

In the end, we chose a platinum band for the base, but didn't want plain rings. One of the samples in the case had intertwining gold of different colors, like ropes twisting across the ring's base. We chose to replicate that pattern, but with a strand of green gold interlaced with yellow gold. The green represented my Irish heritage, while the yellow highlighted Ryan's German ancestry. Ruth suggested a dimpled border across the top and bottom, something she called a 'rope,' that tied it all together.

Once Ruth was satisfied with her handwritten notes, she vanished into the back of the store, leaving us to browse a bit more. She returned a few minutes later with a computerized image of what our rings would look like. Who knew our little Ruth could work a computer?

Our rings were stunning. Ryan ran a finger over

the image, as if touching his ring. I couldn't stop smiling. He cupped my cheek and said, "I love you."

I melted into his arms. Again, the non-crier was blubbering.

Ruth watched from behind the counter. When I finally emerged, she was still standing with both hands over her mouth, her own tears dribbling down her cheeks.

"Boys, I have a lot of people come through this shop, and no small number of folks gettin' married. I sell a lot of rings. You two are about the most perfectly matched couple I've ever seen—and I'm not just sayin' that. You two are beautiful."

Ryan and I shared another look, then he kissed my forehead.

"Thank you, Ruth. You helped make this day more special than I could've hoped." Ryan rounded the counter and lifted the old woman off the ground. She giggled and wiggled her legs in his embrace, once again a young girl in the arms of a handsome man. When he set her down, she beamed.

"You get outta here before I start cryin' again."

I gave Ruth a quick hug, scratched Q's head, gave the rolltop desk one last wistful glance, and then we headed home.

**6**

---

## THE BEACH

A couple months later, the blessed man in brown delivered two small boxes addressed to Michael and Ryan Lowell. We hadn't discussed taking the other's name, and certainly hadn't ordered our rings to arrive that way. I felt Ruth's guiding hand in the ether. However it happened, I couldn't stop grinning like a goofy cartoon character as Ryan took his box and ripped the packaging up.

"Oh…my…God. It's gorgeous," he said, holding the ring up to the window for better light. For a moment, I thought he'd gone a little *Lord of the Rings* on me and worried he'd snap if I tried to touch his 'precious.'

I pried open my box and struggled to bring myself to lift the band. It gleamed against the sunlight in its dark blue velvet cushion. The green and yellow gold leapt off the platinum base, giving the whole thing a sense of life—of our lives—intertwined on the most precious symbol possible.

Precious.

There was that word again. I had to get Gollum's voice out of my head. He was ruining my ring mojo.

Ryan cleared his throat. As I looked up, he placed the ring on his right hand with a dramatic flourish.

"Uh, your right hand?" I asked.

He shrugged. "We can't officially marry until the nine grow a pair."

"What about RBG?"

"Her balls are bigger than any of the boys, but she's only one vote."

I nodded in agreement.

"Besides, isn't the right hand where gays wear a wedding band? Europeans do it that way. It *has* to be right—and gay."

My laugh turned into a snort. "Are you saying all Europeans are gay?"

"If they're not, they want to be. Everybody's doing it." He snuck in a peck on one cheek, then the other, in classic Euro-style. "See if yours fits."

I hesitated.

"What's wrong? Did they mess something up? Ruth will—"

"No, it's perfect," I said. "It's just…I always

promised myself I wouldn't put *this* ring on my own finger. Ever."

His eyes widened in understanding, then both of his hands gripped my head and pulled me into a long, soft kiss. "I'm going to love you for the rest of your life—and mine. Would you allow me to put it on for you?"

I swooned. "How could a guy say no to that? But only to check the size. I don't want to wear it until we have a ceremony."

He pulled back. "Ceremony?"

"Well, sure. I know we can't legally marry, but I still want to celebrate it with our closest friends. They're our real family anyway. I want to write my own vows, to promise myself to you in a way that both makes you proud and turns you into a puddle of blathering mush."

Now it was his turn to snort. "You know snot isn't romantic, right?"

"No sinus drip required—just a good, old-fashioned emotional breakdown in front of witnesses. That's all I need. Oh, and this ring shoved on my finger so it can't ever come off."

He wrapped his arms around me. "Whatever you want, babe. I'll snot for you."

"Eww."

He dug his nose into my neck and rubbed it back

and forth until I felt goo.

"Ugh, that's so gross."

"You wanted it all." Then he actually blew his nose on my neck. "There you go, babe. All yours."

I pulled away. "You are the vilest form of human. Why do I love you? Remind me."

He grinned as he reached up and cleaned my neck. "Because not only do I give you my snot, I clean it afterward."

"Is that supposed to be sexy? A turn-on?" I asked.

"Whatever it takes, babe. Whatever it takes."

The rings went back in their boxes. Ryan placed them reverently on the mantel, like some prize we'd won for all to see. He bent over and kissed each box before walking away.

My Ryan was a mush pit—and I loved it.

As our minds turned to dinner options, I realized something.

I had never tried my ring on.

---

THE WEEK BEFORE MEMORIAL DAY WEEKEND, OUR townhouse was a blur of activity. Rob and Fin had talked us into joining them on their annual trek to Pensacola, Florida. Apparently, there was some sort of gay ritual that involved thousands of our festive flock flooding the beaches to shake their tail feathers. Rob was especially excited about one event on Saturday night, a circuit party. This year's party was being held on the beach, and a giant stage had been erected for live performances and the requisite DJ booth.

"So, a circuit party? What do you think it'll be like?" I asked.

"No clue," Ryan said as he handed me two different pairs of Speedo. Between his chiseled Adonis belt and the tiny pieces of fabric he'd just handed me, I was sure we'd get plenty of attention on any beach, even one filled with deliciously decked-out gays.

"Should we bring anything? I could make lasagna. Maybe some kind of snack food? I mean, I hate to go to a party empty-handed."

Ryan looked up and thought a moment. "That's not a bad idea, but let me call Rob and ask. The fee to get into the party is fifty bucks. For that kind of money, they should have food there for us. They might not let us bring anything in."

Two minutes later, Ryan held the phone receiver away from his ear as Rob's hysterical laughter rang through. "Michael wants to cook? To bring lasagna to a circuit party?" He barely got the last words out before another round of hyperventilation blared through the line again.

"Uh, yeah. Is that not a thing?" Ryan asked.

We heard Rob call out to someone on his end. "You're not going to believe this. They want to know if they should bring food to the beach party."

Fin's unmistakable bass rumbled as he broke out in fits of laughter.

Ryan held his hand over the speaker. "I think we stepped in something. No cooking."

"No need to cook," Rob said, as if reading Ryan's thoughts. "Tell Betty Crocker we'll have a whole different kind of snack waiting for him."

More laughter from the obnoxious other end.

Ryan just shrugged.

I kept packing with eyes downcast; I felt as though our friends had just chastised my good nature. All I wanted was to be a good partygoer. Was that so wrong?

---

Ryan opened the door to the boys' rental beach condo, and we were greeted by squeals of, "Daddy's home!"

Ryan grumbled something sarcastic that didn't match his grin.

"We can't help that you're so much older and wiser than us," Fin bellowed from the kitchen.

Abe darted from nowhere and wrapped the two of us in a tight hug. His teal Speedo barely covered his kibbles 'n' bits, which he promptly rubbed against us.

"You trying to start a fire with that thing? Jesus, I can tell what religion you are. Don't they come in your size?" Ryan was ready to rumble.

Abe slammed his shoulder playfully. "I'll have you know, old man, if it fits, it's too big. The Gay Manual is quite clear on that point."

"The author would know," Ryan countered, earning another slap.

"If only the gays would follow my lead, this would be a much more festive world." With that pronouncement, he gave me a peck on the cheek, twirled a pirouette, and vanished back down the hallway. The only thing missing was a puff of gay smoke in his wake—or would that be a cloud of glitter?

Anyway.

We quickly settled into our room, ate a bite of lunch, and joined the boys for our first tour of the beach. The condo was only one block from the shore, so we were never far from the action.

Boys were everywhere. Even before our toes hit the sand, Ryan and I were nudging each other, pointing at one hottie or another.

When we stood within a few yards of the rippling waves, we looked up and down the miles-long beach.

Rob had told us there'd be a lot of people here, especially for the party, but we were unprepared for the sight. Butts and boobs crowded onto the sand as far as we could see. Tens of thousands of men and women, many wearing or waving rainbow flags, strolled and played in the sand. They came in every color, flavor, shape, and size—and so did their clothing. There were Speedos, of course, but there were also trunks with every print imaginable, and even some Speedos whose trunks were more exposed than was likely legal. Bright T-shirts with equally bright images or expressions covered the melanin-challenged, while bronzed, sweat-coated skin made the sun-touched look even more godlike.

The bay was huge, but the sea of men and women was unending.

In addition to the people, colorful tents and umbrellas dotted the tan landscape. Some were what we expected—space for groups to escape the sun—but others were more commercial. Vendors sold drinks, food, T-shirts, swimwear, and anything else one might want while baking on a beach. We passed a number of walled tents with the word "Massage" painted on one side or scrawled on a sign above the entrance flap. A few of those had more explicit images beside the wording, and I gathered those rub-downs came with a happier ending.

We strolled for over an hour just to get acclimatized, then found an unoccupied plot of land and planted our flag. Yes, Abe actually planted a flag, making a mock ceremony out of the gesture. We were quite official in our land grab.

Rob surprised us by unpacking a battery-powered blender and mixing frozen margaritas. He produced flavor packets with coloring that matched the gay rainbow flags. Grape was my favorite, though I caught shit from the group for preferring a slushie to a true margarita.

That night, fully baked and drained from a day under the sun, we grilled chicken and baked tater tots as a family, then passed out on the couch as Fin watched some military action movie none of the rest of us cared about. Ryan's head rested in my lap, his breathing heavy and slow as he slept. I brushed a few strands of stray hair out of his face.

"Aww. You two make me so happy." I looked up to find Abe staring, a glassy look in his eyes.

I blushed and continued stroking Ryan's hair.

SATURDAY BROUGHT MORE BEACH AND SUN, THOUGH we were careful not to spend too much time exposed to Florida's harsh rays. Rob insisted we needed to pace ourselves if we were going to truly enjoy the party later that night.

Around two o'clock, he packed up the blender and began folding his beach towel.

"What are you doing? Are we done for the day?" Ryan craned his head back toward him.

"We need our party nap. Come on, you two. Everybody up."

I rolled over to face Ryan. We were lying on a massive beach towel. "Party nap?" I whispered.

He gave me the universal, "I have no idea," eyebrow raise, then stood and offered me his hand.

Such a gentleman, even on a beach.

We napped until Mama Bear woke us up around six. Fin had dinner sizzling, and the whole condo smelled like Jamaican spices and beans. Rob was sitting in front of the coffee table in the den when we wandered out from our bedroom. There were several tiny plastic ziplock bags splayed out before him, each with a handful of blue and pink pills in them.

"What's all that?" Ryan asked.

"Party favors," Rob said cheerily.

Ryan and I shared a confused glance.

"It's X—ecstasy to you rookies," Fin's rumble sounded behind us.

I'd never done any kind of recreational drug. Neither had Ryan. In fact, we'd never even thought about it. Hell, I'd only tried alcohol a few years ago, and that first sip occurred purely because I'd been dragged, unsuspectingly, into a gay bar when I still thought I was straight.

"Uh, we're good, but you guys have fun," Ryan said, then turned to me with a questioning gaze. I nodded in agreement and gripped his hand for support. Something about all this felt strange. For the first time, it felt like we didn't belong in the same room with our little family.

Rob scowled up at Ryan. "Don't be a puss. You two didn't drive all the way down here from Atlanta to not enjoy yourselves. Besides, if you don't do anything, you'll be the only sober guys on the beach, and the whole thing will get really boring really fast."

Ryan sat beside him on the couch and stared at the packets. Superman's crest stared up at him from its embossed place on each pill.

He glanced back up at me. "I guess—"

"Yes, you can, and you will," Rob said, handing him a bag with two pills. "One for each of you. No more. You may even want to cut those in half and pace yourselves until you know what it feels like."

Ryan stared at the bag in his hand as though it was a snake about to strike.

My mouth wouldn't work. I'm not even sure I would've known what to say. The whole scene felt surreal. In the two years we'd known the boys, they'd never even mentioned doing drugs. Yet here they were, looking like experts, like guys who did this regularly.

"Do you guys do these often?" Ryan asked, reading my mind.

Rob shrugged. "Pretty much every time we go out. That's, what—every Saturday night?" He chuckled and Fin grunted over the sound of chicken searing.

Ryan couldn't take his eyes off the pills in his hand.

I squeezed onto the couch beside him and gripped his leg.

"What do you think?" he asked quietly.

"I…uh…I don't know. I mean, I've never—"

"Me either." He turned the package over. The back of the pills was smooth and unadorned. "I am kinda curious, and we *are* here with friends."

*Holy shit*. He wanted to try this. My head spun.

*Michael, no, absolutely not. Don't you even think about it. What would your father say? He's a preacher, for God's sake. Forgive me, Father. I didn't mean to curse.* My little angel appeared in an angry puff wearing a brilliant white robe and shimmering golden halo, just like my mental image from child-hood—minus the wings. His itty-bitty arms were crossed, and his head was tilted with emphatic judgment.

*Puff.* The angel's counterpart appeared on my other shoulder, wearing nothing but a sheer red Speedo that revealed more of his massive, uncut cock than it covered. I'd never seen my little devil's, um, devil. Hell, he was hung—and this iteration of him was muscular, bronzed, and ripped. He looked like a cross between Ricky Martin and Marky Mark, two of my favorite lust objects.

*You aren't seriously going to listen to that righteous windbag, are you? You're at a beach party with the love of your life and your closest friends. There's never going to be a safer time to experiment and let go. Loosen that collar a little, kid. You've been good your whole life. It's time you unpuckered your ass and had a little fun.*

*No, no, no. There will be no unpuckering. Your ass is just fine all puckered up. It's hot, really.* I swear the angel blushed. *You know what I mean. You don't need drugs to enjoy yourself. Being with Ryan gives you all the high you'll ever need.*

*But think about it. What if you could get high with Ryan? How much better could sex with him get? Damn, it makes me hard just thinking about it.* Fuck me. He actually got hard and poked out the top of his

Speedo. Was I actually lusting over my imaginary conscience devil?

I needed serious help.

"Babe? You okay?" Ryan's voice made both images vanish.

*Rock-hard Ryan on X. That puckered asshole would never be the same.* The devil's silky voice slithered inside my head. I shivered.

"Yeah, I'm good. Uh, I don't know. What do you want to do?"

"I kinda want to try it. I mean, we're here and all."

I looked down, unsure. "Can I think about it? It's just…a lot."

He gripped my hand. "But you're okay if I try it?"

That surprised me. We'd always done everything together. All for one, that sort of thing. He wanted to try this without me? Whether I did it or not?

I didn't know what to think about that.

"We'll be there. Fin and I won't let anything happen. Besides, Abe will be hovering like Mother Goose." Rob was really trying to sell this.

"Uh, sure, okay. If you want to," I said. "I just…I just need to think about it a little, okay?"

Ryan's face brightened. "Take your time. We won't leave for the party before eleven anyway."

AT ELEVEN O'CLOCK, RYAN, ROB, FIN, AND ABE each popped a pill.

I couldn't do it.

Thirty minutes later, we marched onto the beach where three thousand shirtless men bounced to booming bass that was blasted through massive speakers on either side of an equally massive stage. Colorful lights bounced off a dozen mirrored balls that hung on scaffolding above the sandy dance area. I scanned the crowd and was stunned to find virtually every body ripped and muscled. Every guy was hot. We'd apparently entered some alternate reality where only Hollywood Hotness was allowed. It was sensory overload.

We wove our way through to the center of the throbbing mass. Our shirts flew off. Ryan's hands found their way to my chest, like magnets drawn to metal. He stroked and kneaded, teased my nipples, then reached up and gripped my shoulders, each squeeze matching the pulse of the music. I looked into his eyes to find them wide and dilated. A broad, overly toothy grin was plastered across his face as his head swayed back and forth. He pulled me into him and held our bodies tightly together as we bobbed to the bass, then he planted his lips on mine in a long, hungry kiss.

But it didn't feel like my Ryan.

Sure, his lower lip was still poochy. And yes, I knew it was him, but it felt different—somehow foreign—like he wasn't kissing *me*, but whoever happened to be in front of him.

I know, that sounds dramatic and crazy. He *was* kissing me, and it felt amazing, but it also felt weird. It's hard to explain.

Three songs later, I was thirsty. The guys were now rolling harder than a bad skier tumbling down a slope, and Ryan barely acknowledged me as I slipped free of the dance floor in search of a vendor.

Jack and Coke in hand, I stood outside the mass of men and watched.

The later it got, the louder the music blasted. The night was cool, in the upper seventies, yet every muscle glistened with sweat. Many of the men no longer danced near their neighbors. They danced against them, bumping and rubbing and grinding. Skin flowed to skin. Hands reached and brushed in every direction. Everyone was connected in some way. Lips found their way to other lips, to shoulders, to chests. It was like watching a sea of sexual sensation, rippling and writhing on a bed of sand.

There was only one mood among that mass, only one emotion.

Thousands throbbed with need and desire. Thousands caressed and careened. Thousands stiffened and stroked. It was the most erotic thing I'd ever seen.

And yet, I was outside looking in. I wasn't a participant, merely an observer.

I hadn't taken the pill.

BY TWO THIRTY, I WAS EXHAUSTED. WHATEVER FUEL the Jack and Coke had given me had long since worn off. Now all I wanted was a tall glass of water and a bed. The bouncing bodies showed no sign of slowing. Ryan and the guys were laughing, hands high in the air, as one favorite dance song after another played. We always like the dance tunes with lyrics, something we could sing along to. Wordless techno from Europe had just arrived on America's shores and was all the rage, yet tonight's DJ offered a refreshing mix of old and new.

Ryan was floating on a cloud, and despite my bleariness, I didn't have the heart to ask him to leave. I found a quiet boulder on the edge of the sandy beach and sat with my back leaning against it. The music wasn't so loud, and I had a clear view of both the stage and the undulation of the bay's waters as they rolled onto the sand.

Even the bay was rolling. I was literally the only one not rolling.

That made me laugh.

A voice barked over the speakers, announcing the end of the evening's festivities. The DJ would play one final song to allow everyone to wind down, something like a cool-down at the end of a workout. It was odd that the party's cool-down was even faster and more heavily bass-laden than the rest of the night's music. I would've thought they'd want to cool the guys off as they closed shop. They were only revving them up.

As the last notes rang out, the crowd began to disperse. Guys, mostly in twos and threes, most holding hands or with arms draped about each other's shoulders, slugged their way through the sand toward town. The massive orgy disintegrated into thousands of smaller, more intimate ones. Hands and lips never stopped roaming. It was clear babies would be made that night. Well, the gays would give it their best shot —so to speak.

I found Ryan and the guys lingering in the dance area. Abe was throat-fucking some twink with long sandy hair, while Rob tried desperately to unpackage a bodybuilder he'd acquired. Ryan and Fin swayed to music that only played in their minds. Each of them sucked on the remains of a lollypop—the white stick

"Hey, boys," I said as I approached them.

"Hey, babe." Ryan's voice carried an unnatural drawl. He pulled his sucker out and unconsciously chewed the side of his mouth.

I later learned that move was called Chewy Chewbacca. Apparently, there was something about X that made you chew or suck anything nearby.

Abe was proving that point with his twink. They seriously needed to get a room.

"I'm coming down now. You ready to go?" I turned back to see Ryan tossing his sucker stick in a nearby garbage bin. He ran a hand through his hair. "Shit, I need a shower."

"Hot water's gonna feel like fire," Fin said. "Maybe sober boy should join you."

Ryan grinned at me. "What about it? Care to wash my back?"

I didn't mean to be a wet towel, but I was drained and sick of being bored on the sideline. "We'll see. I'm pretty beat."

"Suit yourself," Fin said, turning to Ryan. "I'll scrub whatever you need. I've wanted to do that for years."

I could barely believe what I was hearing. Fin was hitting on Ryan. No, he was outright propositioning him.

Ryan let out a low growl. "Hmm. That sounds

amazing. I bet your fingers would make my whole body tingle."

*What the fuck?*

"Come on, guys. Let's go." I bit back my rising anger as we left the beach. They were just high. They probably didn't even know what they were saying.

---

ON SUNDAY, RYAN AND THE BOYS SLEPT UNTIL NOON. I'd had breakfast, strolled the beach twice, and souvenir-shopped in the town surrounding our condo by the time they stirred.

"Well, good morning, sleepy head," I said as Ryan appeared in the hallway entrance.

"You're speaking to me. Why are you speaking? Why is anyone speaking?"

I laughed as he squinted his strung-out, still-dilated eyes. None of the window shades were open and only one lamp was on, but he still struggled to adjust. Ah, the joys of the morning after.

"Here, drink this." I handed him my mug I'd just filled with fresh coffee, then turned to the kitchen to pour myself a new one. "Want anything to eat?"

"God, I'm starving. I'll be yours forever if you make me an omelet."

"Last I checked, you're already mine forever. So what's in this omelet thing for me now?"

He let out a weak laugh. "I'll rub your feet, but only after my strength returns."

"Feet for frittata. I like it. Need some toe jam for your toast?"

"I can't decide if I love or hate you more right now." He grinned, both hands pressed to his temples.

"I'll take that," I said in the most annoyingly chipper voice I could muster. He deserved a little torture after his night of frivolity.

The rest of the day was dedicated to recovery. Ryan and the boys laid around on the couch, then took naps. When we finally wandered out to the beach, they clustered under an umbrella with sunglasses glued to their all-too-sensitive eyes. At one point, I caught Ryan with a towel draped across his face to further shield his irises.

We ordered pizza that night. I was the only one not knocking on death's door, and I wasn't up for cooking for my messy men. Four extra-large pies vanished in a blink as the last of the drug's sketchiness dwindled away, replaced by ravenous hunger.

I asked Ryan about his night on the dance floor— dance beach, whatever you called it. He merely grunted and said he'd had fun. He and Rob shared a couple of glances I thought carried more meaning than usual, but I let the subject drop.

Sometimes we Pisces can be too sensitive for our own good.

The next morning, at the butt crack of dawn, we packed up the car and said goodbye to Florida's sunny shores.

# 7

## THE SKY IS GREEN

In June, a simmering pot boiled over.

As you might recall, I'd left my stable, well-paying job at a prominent recruiting firm to start a business with one of my sales guys, Evan. We were both frustrated by our former employer's management style, and Evan had found an exciting opportunity with strong upside and limited upfront investment. I didn't know him well at the time, but he was a decent salesman and a nice enough guy.

What a year in business together taught me was that Evan liked to overanalyze and overthink things more than any human I'd ever met. There was something in the way his brain was wired that required him to examine every conceivable outcome of an action before even leaning in that direction. Don't get me wrong, I'm thoughtful and cautious about decisions, especially if they have broad or long-term conse- quences, but to battle over minor things made me crazy. If I said I wanted to order a box of pens, we'd spend an hour debating the merits of blue versus black ink. If I looked outside my window and commented on how blue the sky was, Evan would crane his neck, then pronounce it green instead. The constant back and forth, our inability to just make decisions and move forward, was insufferable.

In addition to all that, Mr. Amazing Salesman proved to be fairly lazy when it came to prospecting for new business. He was great if I served leads on a platter. He could close anything handed to him. Ask him to go hunt and gather, to find new leads and bring them to the party, and there was a litany of reasons— excuses—why it couldn't be done. As a result, our sales numbers dropped from a healthy flow that paid the bills and allowed us both a comfortable lifestyle to the point where I was juggling which bills would involve loss of power or water if not paid first.

The whole thing was painful and going nowhere fast.

Ryan never said anything, but I could tell my inability to help pay for things was bothering him. He said he understood, but snide comments here and there made me think otherwise. When Rob asked about my job, intimating my business was struggling, I knew my concerns were well founded.

So, in the second week in June, I filed for divorce from Evan. Okay, I quit our company and gave him my half of the ownership, but it felt more like a divorce. Evan was bitter and angry, and I snapped in unprofessional ways that were completely out of character. Going our separate ways was a very good thing.

Ryan said he understood and supported my decision, but immediately asked what I had planned next for employment.

The truth was simple: I had no plan.

The look in his eyes told me he knew it too.

OVER THE NEXT WEEK, WE SCOURED THE NEWSPAPER and online job listings. I wasn't sure what I was even looking for. Sales and sales management had been my role in each prior job, but I wasn't passionate about it. In fact, thinking back, I wasn't passionate about anything I'd done to date. They were just jobs, something to do to pay the bills so I could go out on the weekend or just enjoy life.

What would I love to do if I could do anything?

Ryan asked me that question as we started our search. A week later, I still couldn't answer it.

I could tell his annoyance was growing in direct inversion to his level of patience. The warmth I'd come to expect in his voice was nowhere to be found. I'd heard his businesslike tone enough with his employees over the phone to know he was *managing* me. It felt awful.

Worse, I knew it probably felt awful for him too. He made good money, but with alimony and child support, carrying our entire household was like a lead weight around his neck.

Guilt wove its way in with disappointment and shame.

On Monday of the second week following the break from Evan, I landed an interview with a tech company. I wasn't completely sure what the company did, but the job was managing salespeople, and I knew I could handle that. They could teach me the products or services.

Ryan gave me a halfhearted peck on the cheek as I left our townhouse. He didn't even comment on my suit and tie. The tie was one of the first things he'd ever given me. I tried not to read too much into our lackluster parting and focused on my talking points for the interview.

My meeting with the company's managing partner was to be held in one of those sprawling convention hotels with ballrooms at one end and meeting rooms at the other. I'd never been there before, so I parked at the end with the meeting rooms. Naturally, my interview was in a ballroom.

Ryan always teased me about my sense of direction—or, more accurately, my *lack* of any sense of direction. He quipped I could get lost leaving our driveway, and we lived on a dead-end cul-de-sac.

He wasn't wrong.

The interview went well enough, though I was pretty sure I'd hate working for the asshole who quizzed me. He talked like some Boston elite whose nose was stuck up so high he caught rainwater when he walked outside. He made a snarky comment about my "pleasant" tie, though his voice held only derision as he offered the compliment.

But I needed a job, badly. If it was offered, I'd resigned myself to taking it. I could look for something better while gainfully employed.

As I trudged the length of the eternal series of buildings, I passed through a massively wide hallway where booths had been erected. I'd been so wrapped up in my own head earlier that I hadn't noticed them before. Besides, they'd been empty. Now, they were filled with sharply dressed men and women handing out pamphlets and talking with other sharply dressed people who sat in uncomfortable-looking chairs situated on the opposite side of the booth. I figured there was some convention going on and returned my focus to the pamphlet Mr. Rainwater had given me.

"Are you here for an interview?" A deep voice rumbled behind me.

When I didn't turn, the voice said, "Excuse me, sir."

I turned with a raised brow.

"Yes, you. Thank you." A tall, portly man with a terrible comb-over speared a meaty paw across his table. I shook it, then wiped his sweat on my suit pants.

"Are you here for an interview?" he asked again through a smile filled with crooked, tobacco-stained teeth.

"Uh, yes, well, I was. I had an interview, yes."

I was eloquent.

He chuckled and his whole body rippled. For some reason, I couldn't help liking this man. An involuntary smile snuck onto my face.

"How would you like another?"

Now I was baffled.

"Uh, okay. Sure."

He motioned to a chair and we both sat. Over the

next hour, he introduced me to his financial firm, Waddell & Reed, and how they focused on financial planning for families. He beamed as he spoke about helping people send kids to college, or live well in retirement. He'd been a financial adviser for nearly twenty years and sounded as excited about his work today as he likely did when he'd first started. His enthusiasm and earnestness were infectious.

After a flurry of questions about me and my background, focusing mostly on my sales experience, he explained that he wasn't normally the one conducting interviews, but his boss was short-handed and had asked him to help recruit some talent. He gave me his business card and asked me to call the office and set up an interview with Brad, the branch manager. I smiled, shook his sweaty palm again, and thanked him for accosting me in the middle of a hotel. He made some reference to "mugging for dollars" and we both laughed.

As I finally found my way out the other end of the center, I stared down at the business card in my hand.

*Financial adviser. Huh.* I hadn't even thought of that possibility.

Two weeks and three interviews later, I had a card of my own—along with two insanely large textbooks. The series seven and sixty-six were required industry licenses, and I had to pass those exams before Waddell would start my salary.

Ryan found me buried in the series seven book when he got home that night. He flipped through one of the books, then asked when I had to take my exams.

We didn't celebrate. He never even congratulated me on landing a new job.

8

———

## I'LL COME BACK

On July 2, I passed the series seven. Three days later, I passed the sixty-six. Brad, the branch manager at Waddell, said it was the fastest he'd ever seen anyone pass both exams. I was proud, excited, and slightly terrified. The prospect of starting a new career with a salary that vanished after the first year felt a bit like running a marathon where the track ended on a cliff every runner had to leap off.

Ryan congratulated me on passing with a hug.

The townhouse felt cold and clammy, like some foreign cave I'd wandered into and didn't know whether bears or tigers might dislike my presence in their den. It definitely didn't feel like the home it had been only a few months earlier.

A part of me was dying inside, and I didn't know how to stop it.

On July 6, I walked into the townhouse following a long day of cold calling. Everything was quiet.

"Ryan? You here?" I called out.

"Upstairs."

I climbed the steps and followed his voice into our bedroom. My gut was tight. I didn't understand why, but this moment felt significant; weighty.

Ryan was lying on our bed staring up at the whirling fan. He was still in his business-casual work clothes. He hadn't even taken off his shoes.

"You okay?" I asked from the doorway, unsure if I should even enter our own bedroom.

He didn't even sit up, just turned his head. His eyes were rimmed with red.

I was on the bed in a heartbeat. "Babe, what's wrong? Talk to me."

He stared back at the fan. "I'm sorry."

My gut clenched harder. "Sorry for what? What are you talking about?"

"I can't do this. I'm not ready for forever."

My heart stopped. I couldn't breathe.

His eyes finally met mine, and he took my hand. "I love you, but I'm not ready for forever. I know I'm twelve years older than you, but I'm still new to the gay world. I've never even seen most of it."

I mutely sat for a minute. Then it hit me. "The

party. All the men. You were the center of attention most of the night."

He looked away again. "I've never felt that…I don't know…acceptance. Not from a group like that."

"Ryan, you'll always get attention. You're beautiful. Men will flock to you no matter where you are."

"I didn't know that. I'd never been around more than one or two men at a time."

I leaned back, getting as far away from him as I could while still on the bed. I just couldn't take the closeness in that moment.

"I was married for eighteen years. Diane and I had been together for five years before that. All I've ever known was family and commitment and—" His voice became quiet; small. "There's so much I never got to experience. I didn't get to be young and gay, to go to bars, to just be—"

"To be single." I finished the words he would never have said.

He nodded. "Yeah."

The longest moment I've ever experienced stretched before us. I felt the room widen, a gulf opening between us that had never existed—at least, that I'd never seen or recognized.

I saw it then. It was wide and deep—and insurmountable.

"I need to know what it's like. I can't give my

forever and always look back wondering. It'll eat at me until…"

He didn't have to finish that sentence.

"Michael, I'm so sorry. The last thing I would ever want is to hurt you. You have to believe me. I love you so much."

I saw the agony in his eyes. It mirrored the writhing in my gut. My heart was breaking, yet seeing his torment, I couldn't stop myself from reaching out, from putting him first.

"I know you do."

I closed the gap between us and gripped his hand with both of mine. It felt like holding onto a life vest in the ocean. I knew I was drowning, but there was nothing else I could do. It was there. I had to grab it. I had to pretend it would be alright.

"Babe, I get it. I hate the idea of losing you, but I do understand. I might've been sheltered as a kid, but at least I got to have something of a gay adolescence in my twenties. If I had to do it over again, I don't think I could give that time up, that exploration. It helped me know who I am and what I want."

"I don't want to lose you."

His words stabbed my heart. Anger warred with grief.

How could he say he wanted to see the gay world, to play the field, or whatever the hell he was saying, and then tell me he didn't want to lose me? Those two things couldn't coexist. Could they?

I bit back the bile in my throat and clammed myself. "You're determined to do this?"

He nodded slowly.

"How long have you been thinking about it?"

"Since before Memorial Day. That weekend really put it all into perspective."

*Shit*. He'd been thinking about this for months.

My head spun through the past few months, like watching a movie on fast-forward. There were so many signals I'd missed, so many conversations—or *lack* of conversations. How could I have been so blind?

"I want you to keep your ring."

My head snapped up. "What?"

"Your ring. Keep it."

Our rings hadn't even crossed my mind. Physical things, our townhouse, next steps—none of that mattered in that moment. Why was he bringing up our rings?

"I don't understand."

He finally sat up and faced me. "My plan is to spend a few months going out with Rob and Fin, experience what Atlanta has to offer a new gay, then come back to you."

I pulled away and stood. My mouth was as wide as my eyes. "Ryan, that's not how this works."

He cocked his head like a confused dog.

"You're breaking up with me. You're going to go explore the scene, date, have lots of sex, and likely meet someone new who captures your interest. Even if you don't meet someone special, you'll be focused on what's ahead, not what was behind. I'm behind you now."

He scooted closer on the bed. I took a step back.

"Please, babe. No. I'll come back. We'll come back together. Keep your ring so we can wear them together one day."

I couldn't decide whether I was more amused, confused, hurt, sad, angry—or any of a thousand emotions that raged through my body and mind. I wanted to vomit and run and scream all at the same time. My whole being felt like it was coming apart, yet I was paralyzed.

"In fact, don't move out. I'll take the guest bedroom for now. You won't have to spend money on an apartment, and we'll still be close."

Staring down at Ryan, I realized just how naive he really was about gay life.

"You want me to live here while you explore the gay world, while you date other people? You want me to be here when you bring other men home and have sex with them in the next bedroom? You want me to *see* all that? Seriously?"

I balled my fists to keep them from shaking. The war between grief and anger was taking a decided turn. To end what we had was one thing; to expect me to hang around and watch what followed was beyond rational thought. How could he?

How *dare* he?

"Well, I could—"

"No."

"No?"

"We can look for an apartment. I'll need your help with the first and last month of rent they'll require."

"Of course—"

"Ryan, I *can't* be here. I can't see any of that. The thought of other men—" My voice broke, but I steeled myself for what *had* to be said next.

"Keep the ring. If you ever offer it to me again, please mean what it stands for in your heart. Until then, it's just a pretty scrap of metal in a box to me."

I turned and walked out of our bedroom.

# 9

# THE NEW APARTMENT

Ryan slept in the guest room that night. I didn't ask him to. He just did.

The space next to me felt so empty, a void where such love and warmth once emanated. Now, it held nothing; no one.

I couldn't sleep. When I wasn't crying, I was staring at that damn ceiling fan, the same one that had captivated Ryan so much earlier. Like the anger and pain roiling inside me, it kept spinning and spinning.

Sometime in the middle of the night, I couldn't take the emptiness of our room anymore. Like an idiot —or a man dying of thirst on an island—I found myself crawling into the guest bed beside Ryan. I needed his presence, his warmth, his touch.

Before I knew what I was doing, my lips were pressed to the back of his neck, and my hands were snaking their way around to graze his bare arms and chest.

He didn't move. He didn't even acknowledge that I'd joined him.

Like an idiot, I rubbed up against him, tried to feel excitement—tried to feel *his* excitement.

He remained still.

Eternal moments later, I lay back and stared into the guest room fan. Ryan didn't stir as tears flowed down my cheeks again.

***

I WOKE THE NEXT MORNING TO THE SOUND OF A LOUD motor outside the window. Peeking through the shutter slats, I saw Ryan exit a small U-Haul truck. He slammed the door, and my heart's walls clanged back into place, the same walls I'd let fall completely when Ryan—

Tears. Why wouldn't they stop?

I ran into the bathroom, locked the door, and turned on the shower. He couldn't see me like this. I wouldn't let him see me turn into a complete mess. I wouldn't.

"Hey, everything alright in there?" His knock made me jump from my place on the floor by the sink.

"Uh, yeah. Just cleaning up. Be out in a minute."

The shower had been running for at least thirty minutes. There was some comfort in the sound of its water, in the safety of the bathroom's privacy. I know that makes no sense, but nothing made sense in those moments.

"I got a moving truck. We can load your stuff and then go apartment hunting."

*What the fuck? Who does that?*

It was literally the *next day* following his bomb-drop, the one in which he offered to let me continue living in his romper room while he, well, romped. Now he wanted me out immediately? So much so, he'd rented a U-Haul first thing in the morning?

God, could this get any worse?

In every previous move I'd made in life, packing the moving truck had been a challenge. There was never enough room, and getting couches, chairs, and other non-Tetris shapes to fit neatly was nearly impossible.

We didn't have that problem.

By the time the last of my meager collection was loaded and Ryan slammed the metal door shut, half the truck remained empty. Almost everything we'd bought over the preceding two years had meaning. It was a vase from a trip we took to New York, or an antique dresser we found while in San Francisco. I walked through the townhouse and realized there was very little that didn't tell part of our story. I didn't want to restart life in an empty, lifeless apartment, but I couldn't bear the thought of seeing things that reminded me of Ryan—and our life together—every time I walked through my new home.

Unpacking took even less time than packing.

The Post Apartments had been my home for seven years before meeting Ryan, and they were happy to welcome a wayward son home. Ryan wrote a check for the deposit and first month's rent, then helped me lug my couch and few other belongings up three flights of stairs. When he left, I sat on the floor and leaned back against the couch's leather front.

The apartment was so quiet. I didn't even have a television.

Two moving boxes served as side tables. I was back to using my college silverware and plates, most of which carried at least one chip. My mattress dated back to when my oldest sister still lived at home with my parents. It must've been over twenty years old now, and had more lumps than curdled milk in coffee.

Did I mention the place was quiet?

Well, it was until the world folded in around me and I began crying again. I curled into a ball on the floor of that empty apartment and cried until my throat hurt and eyes burned.

As the sun set, I forced myself to wander

aimlessly into the bedroom and unpack a little. Clothes went into the closet or my mother's old dresser. My one spare pillowcase and set of sheets dropped into the bottom drawer. I'd never been much of a shoe guy, so my one pair of sneakers and dress shoes landed on the floor of the half-empty closet under two lonely suits and three white dress shirts.

I glanced in the closet, then at the dresser's open drawers. My life, such that it was, glared back.

I curled up on the bed, not even bothering to get under the covers. I lay there all night, bouncing between restless sleep and tears I thought had dried.

SUNLIGHT STREAMING THROUGH THE UNCOVERED window woke me at some ungodly hour the next morning. I drifted into the kitchen for the requisite two cups of coffee necessary before conscious thought could occur. I pulled my lone mug out of the cabinet. A set of embossed jail bars stared up at me. Ryan had bought it for me on our tour of Alcatraz. It reminded me of what I'd just lost.

Before my emotions could kick in, I turned to make coffee. The empty space on the counter reminded me I didn't have a coffee maker either.

The mug slipped out of my hands and shattered. That's all it took.

I dropped to my knees, scooping up pieces of broken ceramic, begging them back together as if binding them again could repair more than a simple mug. The pieces wouldn't fit back into place. They were too broken. I became frantic, desperate to make them fit. When they refused, I tossed them on the linoleum, slumped against the cabinets, and wept anew.

Sometime later, with the shattered pieces of Alcatraz still littering the kitchen floor, I mustered the courage to call Brad at Waddell.

"Hey, Michael. Are we going to see you today? We've missed you in our morning sessions."

Every morning, the new financial advisers gathered in the conference room for a "murder boarding" exercise. Anyone who had a new client case would put every piece of information they'd gathered about the prospective family on the whiteboard. The rest of us would poke holes, asking questions in an attempt to discover missing information or determine what more the adviser needed to ask his new client. It was a great training exercise and was mandatory until an adviser's second year in production. I'd missed two mornings in a row without so much as a phone call.

"I'm sorry, Brad. I've…had some personal issues this week."

"Are you okay?" The genuine concern in his voice made my resolve crack.

"I…yeah…no. No, I'm not really." I gasped for air. "My partner ended things. I'm not…Brad, I can barely…I can't—"

"Michael, listen, take all the time you need. This place will be here when you're ready."

"Thanks, Brad. I'm sorry. I need to go."

I hung up and sank into my couch. At least work wasn't pressuring me. That was something.

My next call was one I should've made two days ago.

"Hi, hi, hi!" Connie's ever-chipper voice sang through the receiver.

"Hey."

"Uh-oh. I don't like that tone. What happened?"

"Connie—" I couldn't finish whatever was about to tumble out. I broke down in hysterical tears that felt like they would never end.

"I'm on my way. Don't move."

I gave her my new address, and fifteen minutes later, she knocked on my door. She didn't say a word, just wrapped me in a tight hug and held me as her shoulder became soaked with my tears.

We stood like that for ten or fifteen minutes. I don't remember. At some point, she gently moved me to the couch. The crying ran its course a short time later, but we still didn't speak. She just held me and stroked my hair.

"He said this was forever."

Those were my first words to her.

"I know, sweet pea. I know."

I pulled back, about arm's length, and looked into her eyes. "I get he hasn't been out and seen the gay world. He hasn't done the parties or dating or, I don't know, any of the other gay life stuff. But is all that worth more than a life with me?"

"Oh, Michael, no. Don't say that."

"But that's what he's saying to me, isn't it? How else should I take this? He had a choice, and he chose exploration over love. He chose to be a gay teenager over a married adult—with me. I came in second to parties and drugs—"

"Drugs?" She sat up straight.

My eyes lowered. "Yeah. Guess I didn't tell you about Memorial Day weekend, did I?"

"You talked about the beach and all the men, but never mentioned drugs."

I hadn't told her. I hadn't known how.

Sitting on the couch in the middle of my empty apartment, it all tumbled out.

"Do you think he's using drugs regularly now?" she asked.

"Regularly? Like an addict?"

She nodded.

I shook my head. "No. It's not like that. At least, I don't think it is. His job is way too intense and high profile for him to use and stay on top of his game. That was his first time. I'm pretty sure."

She let out a breath. "That's a relief, I guess. I was worried he'd gotten himself mixed up in something bad."

I half laughed. "I think that's what's next, not what he's already done."

The pity in her eyes was worse than the silence.

WE ORDERED CHINESE DELIVERED TO MY APARTMENT. She ate chicken with string beans while I pushed cashews around the container without tasting a single one. We put the leftovers away. I stared blankly into the open door, cold air blowing across my bare feet. The white cartons with their wire handles were the only items in my new fridge.

Connie left shortly after.

Then the phone rang. Ryan was the only person who had my new number.

"Hello?"

"Hey, baby doll. How are you doing?" It was Abe.

"Guess you heard?"

"Yeah."

I didn't know what else to say.

"I'm sorry." He was never at a loss for words either. Tonight he had so few.

"Me too."

When silence lingered again, he said, "Well, if you need anything, call me, okay?"

"Thanks, Abe." I started to hang up, but couldn't resist asking, "How is he?"

Another pregnant pause. "He's fine. Don't worry about him."

"Is he—"

"Michael, please don't ask."

"Sorry. I'd never put you in the middle, it's just—"

"I get it. You're hurting and want to know what's going on. You want to know why, to understand."

"Yeah."

"There's nothing that will help you understand at this point. Trust me. You just have to get through each day. At some point, they'll just get easier. They'll get better."

I choked a sob back. "Thanks, Abe. I gotta go."

I hung up before the sob took control.

None of our other friends called. Not once.

**10**

———

# HORSEPLAY

I t took me another week to go back into the office. I was numb, staring blindly at the whiteboard as others dissected the willing victim's work. They laughed and teased. The senior adviser at the front of the room egged them on, guiding the discussion through questions and answers the group had missed. I usually loved the banter and exchange of ideas. That morning, I barely blinked as the whiteboard filled with facts and figures.

I'd never felt so dazed.

After work, I forced myself to return to the gym. Guys I hadn't seen in a while waved and shouted greeting. When Ryan and I had moved up to Roswell, I'd dropped my membership in Midtown in favor of a chain warehouse-type facility near our townhouse.

While the equipment had been newer, and the building larger, that place had never felt right. The other folks working out weren't as friendly. They definitely weren't as gay (as if that was possible outside the Gay Bubble). I missed the warmth of the muscle-heads who never failed to encourage that extra push, and I missed the eye candy. Damn, the men of Midtown were hot.

I know, I know. I'd been hopelessly in love. What did I need with eye candy?

Just because I was set to walk down the aisle (at least, I thought I was), didn't mean I was dead. I still had eyes. I still liked craning my neck and checking out a hottie strolling by. I'd never even thought about acting on my unabated lust, but I enjoyed a good drool as much as the next guy.

Plus, smaller gyms were like a family. You might never see the guys who worked out next to you in any other setting, but you felt bonded, joined in a common —and very painful—purpose.

It was good to be back.

Unfortunately, my muscles rebelled at the thought of experiencing strains they hadn't known for weeks, and I had to drop my weights down a few notches just to get through all the sets. I might've been embarrassed if I'd had the capacity to care what anyone else thought right then. I just didn't.

One of the most consistent, friendliest meat-heads swaggered over next to me.

"Hey, stranger. Good to have you back. Where've you been all this time?"

His name, ironically, was also Michael, though he went by Mickey. His neck was bigger than his head, and his legs were thicker than my waist. I wouldn't say I was jealous—that's not a look I'd ever aimed for —but he had muscles layered on muscles, his face was striking, and his smile was infectious. It made for a very pleasant package.

Oh, his package. That was…unfortunate. An itty-bitty wittle wabbit, as Bugs might say.

Steroids might've paved the way to bigger bodies, but they clearly had their side effects.

"Shit, Mickey. It's been, what, a year?"

"Two. You vanished without a trace. We figured you either died or got married. Pretty much the same result either way." He laughed, proud of his own joke. Despite hitting a painful mark, I couldn't help but smile. The dumb ox was just so damn pleasant.

"Yeah, something like that. Kinda got left at the altar. Now, it's just the dying part without the marriage."

I was trying to be funny, to mirror his mood, but it just came out bitter and sad.

Mickey's meaty palm found my shoulder. "I'm

sorry, man. I'm here if you want to talk about it. Really."

"Thanks, Mickey. I'm kinda talked out at this point, but I appreciate the offer."

"Anytime. I mean it." He leaned down and whispered in my ear. "Michael, you're hot as fuck. I don't know the guy who left you, but he's an idiot. It won't take you two minutes to find someone else who actually appreciates how amazing you are. Give yourself time, but don't be afraid to get back out there on the field."

My mouth opened, but nothing came out. Mickey had never talked to me about anything other than weights, muscles, and nutrition. When I looked from his hand on my shoulder into his eyes, the sincerity and depth I found threatened to open my wounds right there on the gym floor.

He must've seen the change in my expression and saved me from an embarrassing scene, reaching down and picking up one of the dumbbells at my feet and offering it to me.

"Now, are you going to lift these or just stare them back into the racks?"

A rebellious chuckle escaped the bonds of my despair. "Right." I grabbed the weight from his hands, then heaved the other one and resumed my curls.

Fuck, that hurt on *every* level.

Please remind me why I liked the gym so much?

---

TWO MONTHS AFTER THE BREAKUP, I CAVED. ABE AND several of the guys at the gym had been hounding me to "get back on the horse," as though getting over a relationship was as easy as jumping into a saddle. I wasn't exactly an expert horseman…horse rider… jockey…whatever, but I knew a thing or two about breakups. It was never that easy.

But Abe was hard to ignore, especially when he went into full pest mode.

It was Friday night. I'd left work early so I had time to hit the gym. If I was going on a date, I wanted to have that good post-workout pump.

Stop smirking! It looked good in a tight shirt.

My dinner date was none other than Mickey from the gym. We'd been chatting a lot lately. He was diligent in checking on me every day when I was working out. His usual opening line of, "What are you working today?" had been replaced by, "You feeling okay today? Anything you want to talk about?" It took a time or two for me to notice the change in pattern, and I wasn't sure if it made me more or less comfortable, but I appreciated his effort and concern.

There was also an element of safety involved. I

knew Mickey. He was a good guy. He wouldn't pressure me or ask for more than I could handle. If I had to mount a new horse, I liked the idea of it being one I knew well.

Oh, and he was hot. I'd never ridden a body-building stud before…er, I mean, horse. Yeah, horse.

We met at Cowtippers. It wasn't fancy, but it was close to home and, again, was comfortable. Every waiter in the place stopped by our table at one point in the night and gave me a warm hug. After the third drive-by, Mickey made a joke about me doing a lot more than tipping cows in that restaurant. His easy smile and quick laugh calmed my jittery nerves.

His steak arrived shortly before my regular Cowtippers meal of grilled chicken and baked sweet potato.

"Look at you being Mr. Healthy Dinner."

I grinned and picked up the two plastic containers crammed with butter, brown sugar, and cinnamon. He watched me dump their contents onto my potato.

"You spoke too soon, my friend."

He chuckled. "So I did. I'm so disappointed now."

"Hey!" I threw my hands up in mock offense. "Kinda harsh there, aren't ya, Ryan?"

Mickey cocked his head. His eyes were…inquisitive? No, that wasn't right. What was that look?

"Michael, it's okay."

Now it was my turn to look bemused. "Um, sorry? I really was teasing about the butter and brown sugar. I know I should be better, but—"

The grin he gave me held no amusement. He had that expression my father used to give me when I was little and got caught doing something, then tried to make up a really stupid, unbelievable story to cover my tracks. It was a knowing look, filled with understanding and a hint of pity. Why was Mickey giving me a piteous look?

"It wasn't the butter, although you really should watch that stuff. Your abs will thank you if you eat your veggies plain." And that smile crossed his face again. "You called me Ryan."

"What? When? Seriously?"

He nodded slowly, his eyes never wavering or leaving mine.

*Fuck. Seriously, fucking shit.*

My eyes plunged to my plate.

A thick, meaty hand covered mine. "Michael, it's okay."

"No, it's not." I was close to tears. "I'm sorry. I shouldn't have—"

"Should, shouldn't…there's no such things. You feel how you feel, and you've been through a lot. I'm just glad we had dinner together."

I looked up and tried to smile through blurry eyes.

He went on. "Someone told you to 'get back on that horse' or 'nothing heals a breakup like finding another man,' right?"

I nodded, once again that little boy unsure how to speak.

"That's shit advice." My head snapped up. He sighed and sat back as his eyes became distant and he traveled to some faraway place or time. "When my partner and I broke up, I cried for a year. It took me another year to date without comparing every guy I met to his unreachable standard. I sat across the table, like you are now, and compared how they ate, held their hands, talked—everything. It wasn't fair to them, and it certainly wasn't fair to me.

"I needed more time. I needed to heal, to remember—and to forget. I know my friends were just trying to help, but that wasn't the right way. If only I'd known that at the time."

Our eyes finally connected again.

The hulking bodybuilder who intimidated so many with his good looks and bulging muscles, the guy whose intense, stern gaze made even the stoutest look away, held only kindness and empathy.

*Dammit.* He was one of the good ones, and I was fucking it up.

"I wish our timing was better, Michael. You're one

of the good ones." He stole my thoughts. "Life doesn't always cooperate, does it?"

He was right. Our timing was terrible.

"Yeah. I know. It just sucks, because…I don't know…I've always liked you, and now—"

"Hey, none of that." His trainer voice was back, strong and commanding. "You don't deserve that and neither do I. Take your time. Get your head and heart back together. Life will offer you whatever it has to offer when the time is right."

His eyes didn't match his stern voice. They were deep pools of gentleness and warmth.

"I think I'd better go now."

I fled to the safety of my car. By the time the door slammed shut, I'd lost any semblance of control. There, in the Cowtippers parking lot, I hunched over my steering wheel and wept.

There would be no more horses for a while.

## 11

## A WALK IN THE PARK

S ummer dragged.

Atlanta was hot far longer than was necessary. When Labor Day rolled around, there was no relief. The only saving grace of the month of September was that it heralded the beginning of the basketball preseason, the time when officials began their training meetings in preparation for the upcoming season. I loved being a referee. It was athletic and required a focus that forced me to shut everything else out. It was impossible to start a five-second count, watch for off-ball illegal screens, and think about Ryan at the same time. Who knew wearing stripes was the cure for breakup agony?

Around four o'clock on the last Thursday of September, as I was reviewing my rulebook in anticipation of a pop quiz at the evening's meeting, my phone rang.

"Hello?"

"Hey."

My heart leapt into my throat at the sound of his voice. Ryan.

He hadn't called me since the breakup. I'd called to hear his voice on his answering machine, like some pathetic loser who couldn't just move on, but we hadn't spoken.

I stood from the couch and paced as far as the scrunchy cord would let me.

"Hey," I said. Idiot.

There was a long, uncomfortable silence. "You want to take a walk?"

Well, that was weird. Out of the blue, he wanted to take a walk?

But I was desperate for his attention. I longed for it. The idea of him calling to take a walk, as insane as it now sounds, gave me hope.

"Sure. When?" I asked a little too quickly.

"Uh, now, if you're free. I've over at Piedmont."

"I can be there in five minutes. Where are you in the park?"

"Sitting on our bench."

*Our* bench. He wanted to meet at our bench. He even called it that.

We actually had a bench when we were together. It's where we'd sit and feed pigeons while pointing out hot boys riding by on rollerblades or throwing footballs. It was a bit voyeuristic, but fun.

Oh. My. God. He wanted to see me, to sit on *our* bench again. Did this mean—?

"Okay. See you in a few."

I was jumping on the couch in my socked feet, hands waving in the air, as the receiver dropped to the floor.

This was really happening. Holy shit.

I had to calm down. Just breathe.

Instead, I giggled and sprinted into my bedroom. I changed into a tighter, cleaner T-shirt and shorts that should likely have been worn by an eighth grader rather than a grown-ass man, but they made that man's ass look amazing, and that's all that mattered.

RYAN LOOKED GOOD. REALLY GOOD. I WATCHED HIM for a few minutes before heading over.

He looked up and smiled. For some reason, his smile didn't reach his eyes. It *always* reached his eyes.

Alarm bells sounded in my head, and I immediately went into Pisces mode, dropping onto the bench and grabbing his arm. "Are you okay? What's wrong?"

He gently freed his arm and scooted over so I could sit beside him with some space between us. "I'm okay. Why do you think something's wrong?"

"Ryan Alan Lowell. I know every expression your face makes. I knew them when we were together, and I'll know them twenty years from now. What's wrong?"

His smile finally reached his eyes. He shook his head and chuckled. "I suppose you do—and always will."

I crossed my arms impatiently. He was stalling something.

"So, I need to tell you something, and I think you're fine—"

"You think *I'm* fine?"

"Please, just let me get this out."

I nodded and leaned back, arms now crossed more tightly than before.

A pair of guys strolled slowly by, chatting about some reality television show. Ryan waited until they passed to continue.

"A few weeks ago, we went to Decadence again. We were, well, decadent. You remember what it's like down there?"

I nodded and tried not to react. It had to be above ninety outside, but I was suppressing a shiver.

"I tested positive."

The whole park tilted on some unseen axis.

"I think you're okay. I'm almost sure it happened in New Orleans, but I wanted you to know so you could get tested, to be sure."

I forgot how to breathe.

He leaned forward and took my hand. His touch was clammy, his eyes indifferent.

Then it hit me. He was there—no, *we* were there—because he felt obligated, not because of any concern for me or my safety, and certainly not because he wanted—

I tried to say something, anything. As much as I'd craved his touch moments before, it now felt like that of a stranger, unwelcome and invasive. I pulled my hand away. He stared down into his empty palm.

"When we were together, did you—"

"No, never. Absolutely never. You were the only man I was with during that time. I would tell you if that weren't the case."

"I would hope so." My voice carried far more accusation than he deserved.

We stared at each other, neither of us knowing what to say. I was trying to figure out who the stranger was sitting on our bench. It couldn't be the Ryan I knew, the one with whom conversation flowed like a river, easy and free. This guy barely made eye contact with me. He stumbled and stammered, grasping for anything to say. This guy didn't even want to be there.

It couldn't be the same Ryan.

He finally found words, just not ones I wanted to hear. "You really should get tested, just to be sure."

"I will." I nodded absently. "But I know I'm positive."

His head snapped up.

"Ryan, if you are, so am I. I feel it in my gut. Don't ask me to explain it; I just know."

"Still…"

"Yeah, I know. I'll get tested." I sucked in a breath to steady myself and stood. "Thanks for telling me."

I didn't wait for him to respond. I left him sitting on *our* bench.

## 12

### IS THAT ALL?

I didn't even have a primary care physician. I was that lucky guy who *never* got sick. So, as promised, I made my way to the county health department later that afternoon. They conducted free HIV screenings, and were supposedly very discreet. I jotted my initials and arrival time on the clipboard where instructed, then took a seat in the waiting room where seven other men and one woman sat. Nine people tried not to look at each other, while curiosity drove their eyes around the room. They were decidedly different: different races, different clothing, different styles, and, in the case of the woman, different sexes.

Yet each wore the exact same expression. We were numb with an undercurrent of terrifying trepidation. Each shared the same questions: Am I? Will I be okay? How long do I have—?

"M.R." a nurse called through the glass divider. It was my turn.

The woman reached out and gripped my arm as I passed. Startled, I looked down. She gave me a tight smile and shaky nod that communicated more than any words ever could.

The nurse led me to a sterile white room with one large chair that had arms outfitted with school-desk-type attachments where a patient could rest an arm.

"You are Michael Reed?"

"Yes."

"Why are you here, Michael?"

My face must've shown surprise or annoyance. I felt both at that question. Why the fuck did she think I was there?

Her voice softened. "I'm sorry. I have to ask."

"For an HIV test," I muttered, as though ashamed of some crime I'd committed.

"Do you have reason to believe you have been exposed, or are you just getting a routine test?"

*Sweet Jesus*. How many questions would she ask before just doing this?

"I…my partner…*former* partner…he just tested positive. He said he thought he got it after we broke up, but suggested I test anyway."

She nodded. Her eyes carried sympathy. The assembly-line nurse was now human. "Michael, I'm sorry, both about the exposure and, well, the breakup."

I glared at my shoes and whispered, "Thanks."

Her hand rested on my forearm. "It's going to be okay. No matter what. Look at me."

I looked up.

"You're going to be okay."

I gulped back whatever was trying to escape, but couldn't stop a furtive tear. She reached up and gently wiped it with her thumb, then wrapped her arms around me and let me cry into her shoulder.

When I'd gathered myself again, she reached for more vials than I'd ever seen in one doctor's office. My eyes went from red slits to saucers.

"Do I even have that much blood?"

She chuckled, caught off guard by my transition from tears to teasing.

"I'll try not to take it all, but you know how we vampires are. Once we get a taste—"

She stretched her lips back and tried to show me fangs that weren't there, then bit the air comically. A laugh escaped my lips. She smiled.

Moments later, blood drawn, I exited through a hallway that didn't allow me to see the kind woman who'd offered me support as I went to visit Nurse Vamp. I never saw her again. I never knew how she fared.

TWO DAYS LATER, I RECEIVED A CALL FROM THE front desk of the health department. They had my results, but would only release them in person. The woman explained the policy had nothing to do with what the results contained. Positive or negative, everyone had to come in to learn their fate.

I hadn't told anyone about my conversation with Ryan or the test that followed. Dwayne and I had drifted apart, time and distance doing what they did best. I couldn't bring myself to tell Connie, either because I was ashamed or because I didn't want to worry her until I knew my results. I wasn't sure. It was probably a mix of both.

So, on a cloudy afternoon in September, I drove back to the health department and was ushered down a hallway into a doctor's office. Unlike the sterile exam room where my blood had been drawn, the doc's office held a large wooden desk, and walls covered with certificates and pictures. It had a decidedly personal feel. When the doc appeared in the doorway, I realized the kids in the pictures had to be his. They were miniature clones of the man in the lab coat.

He looked down at a folder in his hand as he rounded his desk and sat in his oversized leather chair.

"Michael?" He looked up through spectacles without raising his head.

I nodded. "Yes, sir."

He read the file a moment, then set it on his desk and locked eyes.

"The test shows the presence of virus in your blood." His voice wasn't cold, but it sounded like a verdict he'd rendered many times before.

"So, I'm—"

"Yes, you have tested positive for the presence of HIV."

He waited for me to say something. I didn't. I didn't even offer a reaction.

"Are you alright?"

Oddly, I was. With a confident, almost snarky voice, I answered. "I'm fine. Are you?"

He snorted. "No one's ever asked *me* that after receiving this news."

"I knew it before we did the test. In my heart, I knew."

He leaned back. "Why do you say that?"

"Because Ryan was positive. For two years, we shared everything."

I thought it was a statement of fact, as clear as the sun rising in the east. The doc's expression said he wasn't sure what to make of the patient sitting before him.

"Do you have any questions for me?" he asked.

I thought a moment. "What do I need to do now? Please just tell me what I need to know in this moment. I don't want to know about things that might happen down the road. If there are decisions I need to make today, I'd like to be fully informed. Otherwise, ignorance is bliss."

The corner of his mouth quirked at my businesslike tone.

"Well, you need to find a doctor who specializes in working with infectious diseases. He or she will run some tests, likely try to determine which strain you have, then suggest a treatment regimen." He leaned forward again and removed his spectacles. "Michael, you're going to be fine. The medicines these days are fantastic, and new ones come out all the time. The vast majority of patients live long, healthy lives, as long as they adhere to their doctor's instructions."

My confidence shattered. "Long, healthy lives?" I muttered, more to myself than to the doc.

He nodded.

"How long?" I asked.

"I'm sorry?"

"How long do I have?"

He scanned the file, then closed it, as if I'd exhausted my question time.

"You're thirty-two now. If you adhere to your

doctor's orders, I'd give you another fifty, maybe sixty years, give or take." His warm smile curled the deep lines around his eyes, and I knew he wasn't just trying to make me feel better.

He was telling me I'd really be okay.

**13**

———

# PURE INTENTIONS

Work was something of a bright spot in the midst of a dark summer and fall. Once past all my exams and initial training, I'd fallen in love with helping clients, hearing about their lives, and working with them to secure a better future. It felt unlike anything I'd ever known. These people, these families, depended on my advice to be able to retire—and to not outlive their savings once they did. When I stopped and thought about it, the weight of that responsibility felt immense, but was also immensely satisfying.

My first client was Mrs. Betty Walker. I'll never forget her. Brad had an adviser leave the company and had to reassign his accounts. Clients with more assets or who generated more revenue were assigned to his best advisers, while we rookies were tossed smaller fish, often clients who were unresponsive to their previous adviser.

Mrs. Walker was one of my "orphaned account" assignments. She had nearly one hundred thousand dollars in a retail account, all in cash. Our records showed the previous adviser only called her once, and she never returned his call.

Batter up!

It took four calls to get her to answer the phone. She sounded four thousand years old and terrified to talk to strangers. When I finally got her talking, she refused to acknowledge she owned an account with Waddell or to discuss any investment ideas we might have. She actually hung up on me.

The next week, I called her again.

"Mr. Reed—"

"Please, Mrs. Walker, call me Michael."

"Mr. Reed, I don't understand why you're calling me again. I told you I don't want to talk to anyone about any investments."

"Yes, ma'am, I understand, but I'm required to keep calling until we discuss your account. Our company—and the folks who regulate us from the government—won't let us have accounts without knowing our clients. I'm really sorry to bother you, but we really do need to talk. Besides, you have quite a lot of money here, and it's all sitting in cash doing very little for you."

"A lot? How much is a lot?"

*Holy shit.* She didn't even know how much was in the account.

"Nearly one hundred thousand dollars."

Silence.

"Mrs. Walker? Did I lose you?"

I heard heavy breathing, then sniffing. She was crying.

"Mrs. Walker, are you okay?"

"I didn't know she'd left me so much."

I waited, ignoring the dozen questions threatening to spill out.

"When Judith died—she was my little sister—she left me that account. I haven't had the heart to even look at it."

"I'm so sorry, Mrs. Walker. When did Judith pass?"

"Six years ago."

Now I really didn't know what to say.

"She was my best friend in the world. My husband died twenty years ago of cancer. Judith moved into my house that week and wouldn't leave. I tried to be nasty, to make her go, but she was more stubborn than I'll ever be. Without her, I don't think I would've survived losing Ben."

Now I was misting up. All thoughts of accounts or investments flew out the window. All I could think of was this poor woman and what she'd lost, how lonely she sounded.

"Her daughter is all I have left, and she lives out in California. She's seven now. Beautiful little girl."

Seven. Her mother died when she was one year old. My heart shuddered.

"What's her name?"

"Marie."

"That's pretty."

I could almost hear her smiling. "She is pretty. I fly out to see her every few months. She calls me Nappy. It's a terrible name, but she couldn't say Nanna when she was little and it stuck. Now everyone thinks I'm a big napkin or some such."

We laughed together for the first time. God, that felt good.

"You sound very proud of her," I said.

"Oh, I'm more than proud. She's my world now, even if she lives all the way across the country. That idiot father of hers—I never liked him—moved out there to find himself or something." She made a spitting sound. "How do you find yourself? Hell, how do you lose yourself to even have to find your own damn self?"

Her sudden cursing caught me off guard and I

snorted a laugh, then caught myself and covered the receiver.

"Oh, now you got me cussin'. Sorry about that."

I couldn't stop grinning. "It's alright. You're supposed to be able to tell me anything, kind of like a lawyer but without the legal protection. A judge can still make me rat on you if you commit a crime."

She laughed. "I'm a crazy criminal, that's for sure. You rat on me all you like."

"So—"

"How old are you, young man? You sound about twelve."

I couldn't decide whether to be offended or laugh. She had that effect.

"I'm thirty-two, but I look like I'm about twelve. We gingers don't age much."

"Ha. Don't I know it. I was seventy-five, maybe seventy-six, before my pepper turned to salt. We reds are alright."

"Yes, ma'am. That's what I think too."

"I like you, Michael Reed. I don't think I'm supposed to, but I do."

I laughed. "I like you too, Mrs. Walker."

There was another pause.

"What did you want me to do with that money?"

I was startled. We'd been so lost in each other's stories that I'd almost forgotten why I called her.

"Well, honestly, I don't know."

She cut me off. "What do you mean? Didn't you call wanting me to invest or something?"

My grin returned. "I called to introduce myself and get to know you. It's pretty hard to give advice without knowing my client and what her goals are."

"I guess that makes sense."

"How would you feel about meeting? I wouldn't want to work with a financial professional I hadn't actually met. Besides, I'd like to hear more about Marie. You could bring pictures."

"Oh, I don't know about meeting. Can't we just talk about all this over the phone?" She retreated back into her shell.

"We could, but it would be easier for me to show you ideas and proposals in person. Investments can be confusing when we can't look at the same sheet of paper."

"I suppose." She thought a moment. "But I don't want to come into some office. You buy me a coffee down at Starbucks."

I chuckled. "It's a date."

"Oh no it's not, young man. Don't go gettin' crazy ideas." She cackled at her own joke. I laughed with her.

"Yes, ma'am. My intentions are pure, I assure you."

Two days later, I rose from a table in the middle of Starbucks to greet Mrs. Walker. She looked every bit the ninety-four years her profile claimed she was. What surprised me was the man holding her hand as they approached the table. His hair still held some darkness, though the battle with gray was clearly in its latter stages.

"Mr. Reed?"

I smiled. "Mrs. Walker, I'm Michael, remember?"

Her smile was brilliant, that of a girl in her twenties whose heart and mind shone through like the sun. I liked her immediately.

"Michael, this is Pete. He's my boyfriend."

It took everything I had not to gape at my nonagenarian client.

"He's here to…" She fumbled for words.

I grinned. "To keep you safe from the man you're meeting for the first time?"

She nodded. "He'll whoop your ass."

I laughed—one of those out-of-control belly laughs that shakes every part of your body. It just tumbled out, and was the first truly free expression of joy I'd felt in months. Her smile widened as she watched me.

During our conversation, I learned just how

wealthy Mrs. Walker was. She hadn't forgotten about the money in her account at Waddell. She hadn't cared about it. It was a tiny portion of her estate and, as she put it, she didn't need a penny of it. With that declaration, Brad's suggestion of investing for the future flew out the window. That was a dumb-ass idea anyway. At what point in a person's life did that conversation become moot?

As my mind spun for other ideas, Mrs. Walker dug through her purse. Her hands surfaced a moment later with a thick stack of Polaroid pictures. We spent the next ten minutes flipping through images of her niece, then her sister, and even one of her late husband. As we reached the bottom of the stack, I hopped up.

"I'm so sorry. We're in Starbucks and I forgot to get you something to drink. What would you like?"

I returned a moment later with two steaming cups.

"I had an idea while I was standing in line," I said, handing Mrs. Walker a mocha latte and Pete his black coffee.

She took a sip and sighed. "Okay, let's hear it."

"What about sending Marie to college?"

She set her cup down and stared up at me. "What do you mean?"

"Well, from what you told me about her father, he's probably not the most financially stable adult. Your sister passed before she could really build wealth. Have you thought about how Marie would pay for college when she's older?"

Mrs. Walker shared a look with Pete, then turned back to me. "No. I'm ashamed to admit it, but I haven't even thought about it."

"That's why you have me, right?" I gave her my warmest "I'm not a used-car salesman" smile.

She chortled. "I like you, dear, but how can I help send Marie to college? She won't be going for another ten or eleven years. I'm afraid I won't be here for any of it."

The reality of that statement was a two-by-four between my eyes.

"I…uh…yes. Well, I think I have a way you can use the money your sister left you and take care of Marie's college. Your legacy will live on with your niece."

For the next twenty minutes, we discussed how 529 Plans worked. In the end, I told Mrs. Walker that I needed to do some homework and get back to her. Coming up with the idea in line at Starbucks was very different to creating a financial plan with well-crunched numbers to ensure the greatest probability of success.

*Who the hell are you? And what have you done with Michael? And who talks like that?* the little devil snarked in my mind.

*Oh, shut up, Toasty. He's doing the Lord's work here. Leave him be*, the angel retorted.

As strange as having warring voices in my head was, it was good to have them back. They'd been silent since the breakup.

"I'll call you tomorrow and we can go over the numbers. If this works, Marie will never have to worry about paying for her education."

Mrs. Walker's eyes were moist. She rose with Pete's help, then tossed off his hand and bounded around the table to wrap me in a bony embrace. I fell into her arms, returning the hug.

"Thank you, Michael. Thank you," she whispered. "You're a good boy."

---

As promised, I called Mrs. Walker the next day. Everything worked out. With another eleven years to invest the initial hundred grand, Marie should be able to attend any number of excellent colleges without ever opening her own wallet. Through the most beautiful tears I'd ever heard, Mrs. Walker agreed to the plan.

The next morning, the receptionist interrupted the morning murder board session. "Michael, sorry to interrupt. You have a client in the lobby."

Surprised, I glanced at Brad. He grinned. "Go. Clients before training."

I nodded and gathered my notebook, then headed up front. Mrs. Walker sat in one of our puffy leather chairs, mocha latte in one hand and a box wrapped in two kitchen hand towels resting in her lap. I shot forward to brace her as she struggled to her feet.

"Don't ever get old, Michael. Everything hurts when you're old." She gave me the chortle I was coming to love.

"Yes, ma'am. Although, I'm not sure I like the alternative." I winked dramatically.

She cackled again and slapped my arm playfully.

"What brings you into the office? I have to say, I thought Starbucks was our place. You cheating on me with these fancy digs?"

She giggled. "No. I brought you something." She handed me the box. "Go ahead. Open it. I'll take those towels home with me though."

Buried within were homemade oatmeal raisin cookies. They were still warm and gooey.

"You told me you like these, I think. Or it might've been Marie. I can't remember. Anyway, I hope you like them. I just wanted to say thank you. You kept calling when some old lady ignored you, and my baby will go to college because of that. You changed a life this week—two, if you count the old woman who is truly grateful."

My mouth opened but refused to work. I looked down at this beautiful, bent elder and saw such warmth and love in her eyes. One eye couldn't hold back its tear—and that was all it took for my own dam to burst. In seconds, we were wrapped in each other's arms, blubbering like babies. She finally released me, took her towels back, and left the office. I stared at the door for a good minute before breathing deeply and turning to resume training.

The receptionist was staring from behind her desk. Her cheeks were moist.

Brad was leaning in the entryway to the office. He nodded and gave me a proud smile.

That was the day I fell in love with the business.

# 14

## SEASONS OF CHANGE

onths rolled by and life's routine seized control. Days were spent searching for new clients, while most evenings involved either a workout or officiating. I was thankful for the predictable monotony. It kept me busy and unable to be alone with my thoughts too much.

Thinking is overrated when your heart is in pieces.

I worked with a team of thirteen other rookies. We shared a long conference room that had been converted into a bullpen. We called it "the incubator." Card tables lined each wall, and folding chairs spaced every few feet marked out personal space. There were no computers or equipment other than a telephone. It wasn't plush like the senior advisers' offices, but it was all we needed.

I was in my thirties, so I was the old man of the

group. That set me up as the natural go-to guy in the bullpen, the one all the twentysomethings thought knew more than they did because I was older and more mature. That made me laugh, but I accepted the role and mentored as many little chickens as would fit under my wings.

Apparently, Brad noticed. He saw everything.

"Michael, can I borrow you for a minute?" he asked from the incubator's open door one morning.

"Sure."

I followed him into his office. He closed the door behind us—something he never did. My stomach did a tuck and roll. Something was up.

"I have something I want to ask you; more of an opportunity, really," he said as he settled into his plush leather chair behind his sprawling oak desk. I sat down opposite.

When I didn't respond, he continued. "You've shown a lot of initiative with the team, coaching and training where possible."

"They're a good group," I said. "Most of them just need a little guidance. I like helping them."

He nodded. "That's why I wanted to talk to you. There's an opening for a branch manager in Florida. I want you to get your supervisory licenses and take over that office."

I nearly fell out of my chair. "But all my clients

are here. I've only been to Florida once as a kid. I don't know anything about the place." My head was reeling. "Besides, I've never led a team or run a branch. Well, I did run a sales team for a while, but that was different."

"It's not different. Same principles, different products and services." He smiled knowingly. "You're good with advisers, especially newer ones. Most managers aren't. I think you were made for this."

"Thanks, I think." I still couldn't believe what I was hearing. "What about my clients?"

"We'll have to find them a new adviser. Branch managers don't produce. Are you okay with that?"

"I guess. Sounds a little like giving up my safety net though."

Another nod. "That's one way to put it. I've lived without one for two decades now. It's scary at first, but you get used to it. Being in leadership lets you have a broader impact, do more good through more people. If you enjoyed helping that client I saw in the lobby a while back, just think how it would feel to impact hundreds or thousands of families through your team."

Damn, this guy was good. He was pressing all my preacher's kid buttons, hitting me in my soft spot.

"You said Florida. Where, exactly?"

"Sarasota."

"Huh. Never heard of it."

"You don't get out much, do you?" He chuckled. "It's about forty minutes south of Tampa, so you'd be close to a major city, if you like that sort of thing. The office is nice, right on the bay. I'm a little jealous, really."

He pecked on his antiquated computer, then spun his monitor around. The view out a window of a ten-story office building showed crystal blue water spread beyond the camera's vision. The sun was setting, lighting the sky in brilliant hues. The water below reflected that brilliance, like a prism scattering every color of a rainbow. It looked amazing.

No, it looked like home.

I don't know why, but I knew from that one image that Florida would be where I called home for the rest of my life. I felt it. It called to me.

Brad was also right about me loving to coach. I'd always loved coaching and training more than being a player on the field. In my current role, I got to do that without any responsibility for the trainees' performance. That would change, but the idea of spending my days helping others succeed appealed to me.

More than anything, this felt like a fresh start—the fresh start I *desperately* needed. There would be no way to run into Ryan at a bar or the gym or the grocery store if we lived hundreds of miles apart. It seemed the Atlantan fates tried to bump us into one another almost daily, constantly picking at the wounds that refused to heal.

Yes, this sounded good. It sounded right. It *felt* right.

Without thinking further, I looked up and met Brad's eyes.

"If the numbers work, I'm in."

———

CONNIE WRAPPED ME IN A TIGHT EMBRACE, THEN shoved me into my overstuffed car. We shed a tear or two, but her infectious laugh stopped us from becoming blubbering messes in the Post parking lot. I'd miss her. That made this transition bittersweet, but I knew I needed the change.

Sarasota was in the midst of "the season" when I arrived. Locals explained how the population doubled during peak months, as snow birds who lived there half the year arrived and nested. It was a small town, especially compared to a sprawling metropolis like Atlanta, but the slower pace helped me settle in and not feel overwhelmed.

That more relaxed vibe translated into the office environment too. In Atlanta, if you arrived at the office after seven thirty, Brad would greet you with,

"Good afternoon. Thanks for making it in." In Sarasota, we were lucky to see some of our advisers before the market opened at nine thirty.

Another contrast was the dress. Back in the big city, suits were the norm. In Sarasota, suits were nearly akin to religious blasphemy. I tried influencing the dress of my new troops, encouraging them by setting the example, but they just watched me sweat and laughed at the newcomer who was too thick-headed to listen to reason. The teased me, promising my attitude toward ties would change once summer came.

Clearly, I had a lot to learn.

A few months later, I'd established a comfortable routine in my new home. Ten-hour workdays kept me out of trouble. An evening workout at a gym around the block from the office helped me sleep well each night. There was only one gay bar in town at the time. I visited it on my first weekend in town. Of the seven people in the place, six were over the age of sixty. The seventh was nineteen. The bartender gave me a sympathetic look as I scanned the scene, then gave me a shot of something for my trouble. At least the shot was fruity and closer to my age than any of the guys in the bar.

At a loss for where to meet guys, I turned to my most trusted sources: AOL, Manhunt, and

Adam4Adam. Their pages were almost as desolate as the bar had been. I would love to tell you I spent hours scrolling through profiles, creating a whole new binder filled with stars and possibilities, but the bounties of Sarasota eluded me. Well, the single men eluded me. Bounties might be a bit dramatic.

I found a local gym and promised to be diligent in working out. Somewhere in the back of my mind, I held out hope my gaydar would buzz as I watched hotties roam from one bench to the next. Alas, hotties were few and far between, and none of them set off any alarms. One guy who'd obviously enjoyed far too many party drugs in his youth twitched his way over one evening. He used his best pickup line and tried to be witty, but I couldn't see past his hollowed-out eyes and stained teeth. On another night, a man old enough to be my grandfather made a pass. He was handsome and well-spoken, but I had a simple rule: If the wrinkles on the skin make me want to iron, they're too old.

He failed that test.

Sarasota's sad gay newspaper boasted of a softball team filled with athletic hotties ready to pitch and catch. I called the number in the ad and spoke with the captain. They indeed needed a good pitcher, but the season wouldn't start for months and there was no off-season ball to be played. I'd hoped to make some friends, maybe even find a date or two from the team, but that grape died on the vine.

There was this one guy who lived in Palm Beach. His name was Pedro, and he'd immigrated from Cuba when he was two. We met on AOL, chatted a few times, then I drove three hours to meet him and his two greyhounds. Pedro was hot and spicy, and I liked him well enough, but the idea of driving three hours for a date got old quickly. After three weekend visits, I called it quits.

After Pedro, I gave up on the dating scene and turned to my favorite pastime: basketball officiating. There was a local officials' association, but the territory they covered was ridiculous. There was no way I could work a regular day in the office and make it to a high school basketball game in time. I was eighteen years old when I stepped onto a court in stripes that first time. After a twenty-year career, the last thing I wanted to do was hang up my whistle, but I didn't have much choice. The distance and timing wouldn't cooperate.

Now I really was at a loss.

And I was lonely.

Ten-hour workdays turned into twelve. Healthy, home-cooked meals morphed into Chinese takeout and order-in pizza. I tried getting into *American Idol*

and other shows the folks at work talked about incessantly, but none of it charged my batteries.

That's when it hit me.

I needed a friend, one who would be there no
matter what, who would love me and welcome me
home with open arms.

*Dammit.* That made me think of Ryan—and I
hadn't thought of him once since moving. There
endeth the streak.

No, I actually wasn't thinking about dating or men
at all. I needed a dog!

The internet provided an endless stream of advice
on which breed was best for apartment living, so I did
what any self-respecting guy would do—I ignored all
of it. When my eyes fell on a black lab, my heart
soared. Black lab it would be. It *had* to be. I'd name
him Smoky or Jet. If she was, well, a she, I'd name
her Blanca.

*You know that means "white," don't you?* The
angel appeared in white shorts and a white T-shirt
holding a red leash in one hand, as if ready to walk my
soon-to-be pup.

"Yes, I know that. It's ironic—and that's a very
gay thing to be," I said out loud, suddenly self-
conscious to be talking aloud to my conscience.

*You need therapy, not irony.*

"Ha ha. I'm not the one holding an empty leash for a dog we don't have yet."

*This leash is for you. New town, new rules. No more wild Michael. You've sown your oats. Now you need to be a good boy like your mama raised you, young man.*

"You've gotten so bossy in your old age."

*Old? You have no idea how old I am. Angels—*

*Oh, shut it. You're ancient and wise. We get it. If you'd stop badgering the boy, he might get laid. I think we can both agree he would be far more enjoyable after a good pipe fitting.* The devil made his dramatic entrance in red leather riding breeches and red boots. Oddly, he was shirtless and bore rippling muscles and sculpted abs. Holy shit, he looked hot.

*Did you just ogle your imaginary friend?* the angel mocked.

*He sure did,* the devil said, flexing like Arnold. *Look at these guns. You know you want some, wing boy.*

"Are you two done? Jesus."

*Easy with that name,* the angel scolded.

"Fair enough. Now, go away. I'm heading to the shelter to find Smoky or Inky or Blanca."

*That poor animal,* the devil said as he vanished in a puff of red mist.

---

Hours later, I'd seen every dog the two shelters in town had to offer. It broke my heart to leave them in cages, but there weren't any black labs and I was committed to Licorice.

Okay, that would definitely not be his name.

The next weekend, I visited the same shelters. They'd told me to check back regularly, and we PKs were good at doing what we're told.

Ha, who was I kidding? We're good at *being seen* doing what we're told. Watch out when you're not looking.

Anyway. Round two was also a bust. But, as I was leaving the second shelter, the woman who'd escorted me through and introduced each dog recommended I drive a little south to the shelter near the county line. Sarasota was a long county, much like its beaches, and there was a whole other world at the southern end of town. My dog search was turning out to be educational. I thanked the helpful herder and drove twenty minutes to the last stop of the day.

The SoCo Animal Shelter was small but very tidy. It only took a few minutes to see every dog and puppy, even a few cats. I didn't want a cat, but they were fun to play with if I couldn't find a dog. As I was leaving, shoulders slumped at another weekend's failure, a voice called out behind me.

"Michael?"

I turned to find a young woman in her twenties, hair pulled back in a ponytail, wearing the tan pants and light blue shirt of a shelter worker.

"Hi. Yes, I'm Michael."

"I'm Deena. I know you were looking for a black lab, but did you get a chance to meet Jesse?"

I cocked my head. "Jesse?"

"Yes. She's a retriever/chow mixture, reddish tan with the shadow of a black diamond on her head and black liner around her ears. She's beautiful and really sweet."

"No, I don't think I saw her, but I'm—"

"I know. You want a black lab. Would you at least come meet Jesse? She's been cooped up all day and I'm sure she'd enjoy a visitor."

I didn't have anywhere to be, so I acquiesced and followed Deena back down the hallway to the kennels.

"Go into that greeting room. I'll bring Jesse through the staff door." She turned toward the kennels, then turned back. "One thing—Jesse was brought here by a family who couldn't keep her. The parents divorced or something. We never got the full story. She's been sad and hasn't liked many people. Don't be offended if she doesn't let you pet her."

"Okay," I said, even less interested in this visit than before. That was all I needed—a dog who didn't want me back. Sounded too much like my dating life.

*Ooh. Bitter, party of one. Your table is ready.* The devil's silky voice chided in my head. The angel actually snickered.

Rotten, disloyal conscience.

The greeting room was simple and plain; the walls painted white, with dusty white tiles on the floor. Two rickety-looking chairs sat facing each other about six feet apart. I sat in one and waited.

Moments later, the door handle rattled and Deena walked through and sat in the other chair. Jesse sat politely in front of her, still tethered by a leash to Deena's hand. She was a beautiful dog with bright, clear eyes, a keen intelligence shining through. She eyed me, weighing and assessing.

Deena didn't speak, just looked at me, then down at Jesse.

Jesse didn't speak either.

This was going great.

I did the only thing I could think of. I sat on the floor in front of the chair and looked up.

In a flash of fur, Jesse bounded free of Deena's grip and tumbled into my lap. She sniffed my chin a moment, then fell onto her back and nuzzled into my stomach. I was so caught by surprise that I started laughing. That encouraged the pup. Before I knew what was happening, a slobbery black-and-purple tongue was slathering my face. It took a couple minutes for the two of us to calm, but Jesse eventually drew back and sat dutifully by my side, staring up with deep golden eyes. My heart lurched at her unerring gaze.

I'd wanted a black lab, but sometimes what I wanted and what I *needed* were very different things. Life had a funny way of sorting all that out, if I'd just listen.

When I turned from Jesse to Deena, she said six magic words that I'll never forget:

"I think Jesse just adopted you."

**15**

_______

# MERGERS AND ACQUISITIONS

Two years in Sarasota flew by. When I wasn't working eternal days, Jesse and I were walking through downtown or along the bay. She was my constant companion. She also proved to be one of the most well-trained furry friends I could've found. According to the pound, her previous owners raised her from a pup. They guessed her age around two. What the shelter couldn't have known was how much effort they'd put into her training. She knew commands for everything one might imagine, and her keen intellect craved more training and knowledge. With only a few attempts, she quickly picked up on hand signals to accompany the verbal commands she already knew.

There was something in the training process that bonded us in a way I'd not experienced with a dog before. She looked at me differently. It's hard to explain. I'd fallen in love with her the day we met, but when she looked at me with her unfettered, unlimited emotion, I melted. Jesse enjoyed attention and affection, but generally wanted her own space when it was time to stretch out for a nap. The only time she'd break that pattern was when she sensed I was down. Nothing could separate us in those moments. She'd crawl onto the couch and lay her head in my lap until she knew I felt better.

How can animals move our hearts so?

As a tourist town, most restaurants featured outdoor seating that allowed for pets. We became regulars at the dozen or so shops situated within walking distance from my condo. Every server and owner knew Jesse and greeted her by name, usually with a treat from the kitchen or bowl of clean water. People at nearby tables marveled that I never had to give her verbal commands. A quick gesture had her sitting or finding a comfy spot to stretch out.

I might not have had much of a dating life, but I definitely had a best friend.

THE DAY BEFORE MY SECOND ANNIVERSARY IN Sarasota, I got a call from the corporate office. A position had opened to run a nationwide business for the firm based in Tampa, just up the road. They thought I'd be a good fit and wanted me to post for the role. It was something of a hybrid between running a branch and a massive call center. Brad, my former boss and now mentor, told me I was crazy to even question the opportunity.

Two weeks and six interviews later, I got the job.

Four weeks after that, Jesse and I said goodbye to Sarasota. We'd enjoyed our time in a small beach town, but I was looking forward to living in a bigger city again.

At thirty-five years old, my gay biological clock was ticking. Online, guys were already filtering me out in their searches. A twentysomething viewed anyone with a three in front of his age as ancient. Heaven forbid that number started with a four! It was like I was aging out of a dating game show. The same guys who'd hit on me at a bar would avoid me online because I fell outside their age search criteria. It was definitely a new wrinkle I hadn't expected.

Being HIV positive hadn't exactly made things easier either. I'd been lucky, never once experiencing any symptoms or variations in blood counts, some-thing my doc credited to clean living and good genes. He said there was something in Irish genes dating back to the potato famine that gave us a sort of resistance to certain things. I never fully understood—or bought—that explanation, but two different docs pointed to studies in the *Journal of the American Medical Association.*

Bless my lucky charms.

Despite being healthy, some guys couldn't wrap their heads around dating a positive man. Honestly, I knew how they felt—I'd been there with Donny. The fact I was experiencing the same fear and rejection that I'd given him weighed on my heart. But I was kind to myself, and the guys, as well. HIV *was* scary if you didn't have the knowledge and life experience. And me, old man that I was, had racked up plenty of each.

I made it a practice to always tell someone up front, before we ever went on a date. There were two reasons. First, it was honest and felt like the right thing to do. Second, and more personally important, it let them run away before I could develop feelings. I hadn't always been so quick to tell my status, and I'd had my heart squished a time or two. That was a hard lesson to learn.

My hope was Tampa, a much larger city, would offer a wider variety of men, as well as a population of guys who had friends or exes who were also positive. I'd found those with even a little experience were less likely to run.

After a week of searching, my agent and I found a house I couldn't live without. The people of Seminole Heights had nicknamed it "The Castle on the Lake" because it was styled after a Spanish castle and sat at the top of a circle drive that wrapped around a small duck pond. A stonemason had built the house in 1923 for his wife, and his work was impeccable. I fell in love with the original hardwoods and tightly fitted marble the moment we walked through the door.

OVER THE NEXT COUPLE YEARS, I DID ALL THE THINGS a gay in his new town would do: discovered all the bars, explored eateries and hangout spots, joined the gay softball league, and created new profiles on every dating app imaginable.

The bars were filled with cute boys in tight jeans. For the first time in my life, I felt old staring at their unlined faces and pubescent bodies. Don't get me wrong—they were hot. I wouldn't throw any of them out of bed—and didn't—but the idea of dating someone so much younger made me pause. All they wanted was to party, to have fun, to shirk responsibil-ity. I had a career now, a real job I loved, and a life I wanted to build. I'd been single for nearly nine years, but I still craved companionship.

Had I become…*an adult*?

The thought made me shudder.

*Get over it, Peaches. We all age.* The devil appeared in a puff, bent over a walker with faux gray hair and spectacles. He was still shirtless with rippling abs and arms. *Well,* we *don't actually—we're eternal. But you lot do. Just slap some cream on it and go find a boy to slap. It'll make you feel younger in minutes— assuming you can last that long, given your advanced age and all.*

"I've found plenty of boys. I think I need some-thing more now."

*Oh shit. Emergency! Emergency! Angel, we need you, now!*

The angel appeared with a toothbrush in his mouth and rollers in his freshly permed hair. He wore a white robe with pink frills at the collar and cuff.

*Wha's wong?* he asked before spitting out his toothpaste.

*Our boy is trying to be responsible. I think he's— wait for it—growing up.*

"Ha ha. You two are hilarious."

*I still think you need to get laid. Let some muscle daddy fuck the second-guessing right out of you. It always worked before.*

The angel sighed. *Oh, Michael, don't listen to him. He's like a rotten tooth, always wanting more sweets but ready to snap the next time you bite down hard—*

*Hard, right. That's what I said. He needs to get hard, then take it hard.*

"You two aren't helping, you know that, right?"

*Fine. Figure it out on your own. I still think you need some dick, stat. Nothing puts you in a better mood than having some dude shove—*

*I believe he gets your point.*

*I'd rather he get some hot guy's point.*

"Enough!" I waved my hand and the pair vanished. "I can't think with you two around."

*My plan didn't involve thinking,* the devil's distant voice rang in my head.

The freakin' angel laughed.

I hated those two sometimes.

# 16

## SERENA V. GENERAL TSO

Part of giving up on dating involved deleting my Manhunt, Adam4Adam, and Grindr profiles.

Yes, I'd become a Grindr aficionado. It was basically the same guys that were on the other sites, only more convenient as an iPhone app featuring proximity and other pertinent details when an, um, immediate need arose.

That makes me sound like such a slut, doesn't it?

*If the slipper fits, Dorothy,* the angel's verbal whip cracked in my head.

Let's ignore him for the moment.

I deleted those profiles, and removed the apps from my phone. I also cleared out the history tab on my computer and removed them from the favorites bar at the top of Internet Explorer.

Sheesh. Everywhere I turned were little drop-pings…drippings…never mind.

*You look good in glittery red shoes. Keep that pair.*

I really needed a therapist.

Bottom line (and no, that was not a sexual refer-ence, you deviant), I was freeing myself of my slutty ways. In fact, I was giving up on men altogether. None of my efforts were yielding more than one- or two-night stands, and I needed to devote more time to my fancy new job anyway. Guys were a distraction to my future success.

That brings us to a Sunday in early September, nearly seven years AR (After Ryan, please keep up here). I was stretched out watching TV, with Jesse sleeping peace-fully on the other piece of sectional, when my phone lit up. If any of this sounds vaguely familiar, it's because it's almost an exact re-creation of my first date. You know, the one that started me on this insane, dark path?

This time, however, it wasn't a call from my roommate's friend. It was an alert from Facebook.

*Huh.* Facebook sent alerts. I hadn't known that.

I'd just signed up for Facebook a few days earlier, determined to replace my Slutisha ways with the more wholesome "share pics of your pups" social network-ing. I hadn't paid much attention to all the bells and whistles when installing the app on my phone, but there was, apparently, a setting that allowed Facebook to send alerts when friends posted pictures or changed information on their profiles.

I stared at the notice, debating turning that feature off, but something about it made me pause.

*Your friend, Pedro Ramirez, just changed his status.*

His status? What did that mean? And when did I friend Pedro? I hadn't seen or talked to him in nearly a year.

Curious, I clicked the alert. Pedro had changed his relationship status to "single."

Oh, that made more sense now.

Wait, Pedro had been dating someone?

I clicked again. He'd dated a guy named Heath for two months. Pedro hadn't posted any explanation for the breakup, nor had he trash-talked his ex. He simply posted a picture of himself and the greyhounds at the park. They spent more time at the park down the street from his house than they did in his house. It was kinda cute.

Now invested in this tale, I noticed Heath's name was a blue link, so I clicked it.

*Holy shit*. Heath was hot.

The first thing I noticed was his ridiculously white smile. The picture appeared to be a selfie taken outside a gas station or store, but the guy's smile was model-perfect.

Then there was his hair. I'm normally more of a chest and arms guy, but Heath's hair game was on point. I couldn't help but stare with envy. Dark, messy locks sprouted in every direction, giving the impression he didn't care that his hair was disheveled, while having placed every strand in exactly the right place.

Deep pools of rich brown smiled almost as brightly as his teeth.

I swooned a little, right there on my couch.

Jesse's head popped up as she glared accusingly.

"I know. You're right. I gave up on men. But I can still look, can't I?"

She gave me a low whimper, then laid her head back down.

I scrolled through Heath's profile. He had a ton of pictures—mostly impromptu shots—all with the same impeccable smile and infuriatingly sexy hair.

Despite his handsome appearance, there was something different about Heath. He seemed genuine, more down-to-earth and grounded than many of the guys I'd met lately. Yes, that was ridiculous to read from a picture or online profile, but it's what I saw.

On a whim, I clicked the Messenger button and sent:

**Michael Reed:** *Hey. Really nice smile.*

I locked my phone and dropped it on the floor before Jesse could judge me.

Seconds later, it chirped.

**Heath Cox:** *Cute smile yourself.*

That was fast. He liked my smile. I grinned into the phone.

**Heath Cox:** *How do you know Pedro?*

*Holy crap.* How had he connected the two of us?

**Heath Cox:** *I saw him on your friends list. He's our one friend in common.*

*Oh.*

**Michael Reed:** *We dated for a minute. The long-distance thing didn't work as well as I'd hoped.*

**Heath Cox:** *Yeah. I moved there, but that didn't make it work any better. He's a good guy, just a little scattered. Loved his dogs though.*

**Michael Reed:** *Did he take you to the park?*

**Heath Cox:** *LOL every night. You too?*

**Michael Reed:** 😊 *Yep.*

**Heath Cox:** *What are you doing right now?*

Well, that was fast. I thought Facebook was a safe zone. *What the hell?*

**Michael Reed:** *Nothing. Kinda bored.*

**Heath Cox:** *Want some company?*

Jesse sensed something in my mood and growled.

"Oh, hush. Daddy might get some dick today. We'll both be better for it."

She huffed and turned away.

**Michael Reed:** *Sure. I guess.*

**Heath Cox:** *One requirement. Do you have the Tennis Channel?*

**Michael Reed:** *Uh, maybe. I'm not sure.*

**Heath Cox:** *Serena's playing in the Open today. No Tennis Channel, no Heath.*

I fiddled with the remote, scrolling through the search function I'd never used. ESPN, ESPN2, ESPN3, Sports South, and a dozen other sports channels, but no Tennis Channel. I found the icon, but a message popped up informing me the Tennis Channel was a premium service that required an additional subscription. There was a button there to subscribe.

Did I *need* the Tennis Channel? Of course not. I didn't even like tennis. But there was a hottie willing to come over if I could flash him my Serena. I clicked "subscribe now."

*I thought you were giving up men.* The angel appeared, accompanied by a blinding flash of light I'd never seen before.

One thump later, he flashed again and vanished. His righteous indignation rang in my ear.

**Michael Reed:** *Oh, found it. Sorry, it was hidden among all the other sports channels.*

Damn, I sounded like a jock. What a stud.

**Heath Cox:** *Tennis is the only real sport. Send me*

*your address. The match starts at two. I'll be there at 1:59.*

* * *

AT PRECISELY 1:59, THE BRASS BELL HANGING BY MY door rang. The back door was propped open with only the interior gate shut to keep the dog inside. Jesse launched herself from the couch and skidded to a halt just beyond the metal bars. Her guttural growl echoed throughout the stone entranceway.

Jesse was a sweet baby, but the chow in her could frighten the manliest of men. More importantly, she was a better judge of character than any animal—or human—I'd ever met. If she didn't like someone, they would never get to stand or sit next to me without her furry ass in between. Her eyes would *never* leave them, and she'd be ready to strike should the need arise. Daddy was well protected from suspicious characters.

If I'd only listened to her more, I would've avoided some really bad second and third dates along the way. A time or two I was sure she'd given me that "I told you so" look after a messy ending. She really was brilliant.

"Come on in. I'm just putting the match on," I

yelled from the couch, grinning at the thought of my magical beast sizing up another meal—I mean, man.

The hinges squealed, and Jesse's growling silenced. I heard her breathing change from threatening to thrilled. When I peered over the couch, all I saw of my pup was her paws in the air. Heath was on his knees, bent over tickling the shit out of her. It sounded like they were both laughing hysterically.

I stood and gaped, unable to process the scene. "Jesse?"

They both looked up, both with a tongue lolling out the side of their mouth. If I hadn't been so shocked by her sudden change, I would've registered how insanely cute the image was.

"I think she likes me," Heath said.

Jesse's head snapped from me to him, then she pawed him to tickle or wrestle—or whatever you'd call what he was doing to my poor, easily manipulated dog.

Okay, maybe not easily manipulated, but it was impressive.

"I'd say so. She doesn't usually like anyone but me."

He beamed. "You just hadn't met *me* yet."

His teeth were just as perfect in real life, gleaming brilliantly like neatly pressed sailors in a row saluting up at me. My "I've given up on men" heart fluttered a bit. I swallowed down the feeling.

"Uh, I can leave you two alone if you need some time, but the match is about to start."

Heath leapt up faster than I thought his six-foot-one frame would allow.

"Sorry, pup, Serena's my girl." He mussed her head then strode through my dining room like he owned the house. "Hey. I'm Heath."

I wasn't sure whether to shake hands or hug or what. Did one do any of that before a tennis match? Was there etiquette for this situation?

Being a complete dork, I waved, as if he were standing in the house across the street rather than two feet away.

He grinned again, then pulled a hand out of his pocket and waved back.

*Fuck.* He'd out-dorked me—on purpose. By the shit-eating grin on his face, he knew it too.

Shit, his grin was cute.

Without another word, he bounded around me and fell onto the couch. Serena had just won the coin toss and was bouncing back to the baseline to begin her warm-up.

Serena fought valiantly against Victoria Azarenka.

I wasn't into the tennis, but my guest was fascinating. He hung on every point. Actually, that's not accurate. He hung on every shot, every movement, every step Serena took. He went on about her "tiny step" as she approached the ball, her balance as she set up, and the easy power she got from her hip rotation and follow through. Every aspect of the game excited him.

I understood that she'd won, that's about it.

Don't get me wrong. I was athletic and played softball, and the basic mechanics of sport made sense to me, so I could follow most of what he said, but I'd never viewed tennis as being all that complex. Get the ball back. Wasn't that all there was to it?

Oh no. Tennis is freakin' hard. The more I listened to him, the more I realized tennis was a team sport wrapped in an individual effort. One person doing things ten should be doing—all at once. It wasn't only complex, it was incredibly difficult. The level of athleticism and coordination required to be decent was incredible. I couldn't even fathom the skill it took to be a professional.

And then there was Serena. There really wasn't anyone on her level. She played on a different planet from everyone else.

That's how Heath described it.

Between the first and second sets, when we realized the match would go much longer than expected, Heath asked if I'd had lunch.

"Uh, no, I hadn't even thought about it until now. I am kind of hungry."

He looked at me expectantly.

I ran a hand through my hair. "I, uh, haven't been to the grocery store in a minute. Mind if we order in?"

"No, that sounds great." He flashed me those damn teeth again. I tried to look away, but they were eye magnets, some form of demon magic pulling me into their deep brown eternity.

"Uh, okay, well, Chinese?" Fuck, I was stammering.

He grinned. "Sure. White meat only, please. General Tso's Chicken."

"Got it."

Thirty minutes later, we were at the "business end" of the second set. That's what Heath called it. Apparently, shit got real in a tennis match when the score reached 4–4. I didn't understand why, but sat forward on the couch, mirroring Heath, as though it was the most exciting thing ever.

*You really don't know anything about this. You just want his cock,* the devil snickered in my head.

"Shut it. I'm a little busy here," I whispered.

"What?" Heath said through a mouthful of spicy chicken goodness.

"Oh sorry, was somewhere else."

He cocked his head like a confused puppy, but turned back to the match.

*Get this dumb game over so we can get him naked.* The devil was persistent today.

"Yes!" Heath yelled at the television, masking my, "Fuck off," to the devil.

I caught myself watching him a little too openly a few times. He sat, leaned forward, literally on the edge of the couch, arms waving or clapping each time the chair umpire called the score. The tiny lines around his eyes curved upward when he smiled. A few rebellious curls kept falling into his face, forcing his hand up to brush them back. His fingers wove in the locks and slowly dragged them back.

Why was that simple act so sensual to me?

His eating *wasn't* sensual, by any definition of the word. In fact, he shoveled chicken and rice into his mouth so fast I wondered if he was bored with me and wanted to be done with our impromptu date. In a flash, his cartons were empty and cast aside, and his attention had returned to the match.

I beat my insecurities into submission and chalked his ravenous ways up to excitement over a great match.

I couldn't stop peeking as he roared at the screen.

Serena won in a thrilling third set. Heath was elated.

Then I looked down and realized Jesse had curled up on the couch at his side and fallen asleep, completely ignoring his outbursts and wild gesticulations. He'd been petting her throughout most of the match. She hadn't even sat between us—and she never let *anyone* touch her while she slept, rarely even me.

**17**

---

# POST-MATCH RECOVERY

I picked up our plates and the leftover Chinese food containers while Heath rattled on about the match. It was cute to see him so excited. He hopped up from the couch and showed me a few moves, imitating Serena's forehand with surprising precision. When he tried to imitate her tiny steps, he made a *dat-dat-dat* sound with his mouth that cracked me up. He wasn't just into tennis, he was goofy-funny into it.

He compared the match we'd just watched to ones from the '70s, then explained how Steffi Graf was his all-time favorite player. There was something about her slice and movement. I think he said, "Her motto was, 'Hit it where they're not.' When they return it, hit it to the other side where they're not." That actually sounded like something I'd say as I tried to dumb down a very complicated sport.

Jesse had followed me dutifully into the kitchen, probably hoping Daddy would drop a few chunks of chicken. He did not. She then gave me the unmistakable signal that she needed to go potty.

"Hey, Heath. Want to take Jesse for a walk? Looks like she needs to do her business."

He dropped to the kitchen floor and she flopped into his lap, gobbling up every ounce of loving he offered.

I rolled my eyes. "You're such a slut!"

She looked up and grinned, understanding every word I'd said and claiming them.

Heath laughed as he wrestled her.

I shook my head. It was clear he'd won her over.

"Looks like I've won her over. What do I have to do about her dad?"

*Holy shit.* Was he in my head? And did he just say he wanted to win *me* over? A little tingle I'd thought long gone traveled up my spine.

"Uh, well, right now a walk would be good."

Why was I suddenly nervous?

We strolled around the pond. Turtles sunbathing on logs stretched their wrinkly necks as we passed. Ducks paddled toward us, likely hoping we'd brought an offering of bread. They were the fattest ducks on the planet thanks to the constant feeding by those of us who lived around the water. Heath drank it all in.

Oddly, Jesse insisted on walking by *his* side. I finally handed him the leash so we'd stop having to change places each time she crossed our paths with her nylon tether.

That furry little traitor.

"So, what now?" Heath asked as I unclipped Jesse's leash in the doorway.

When I looked up, he was leaning against the wall in a way that pulled his shirt across his lean, muscular chest. A thick forest of black hair tried to escape out the top. His sleeves had rolled up slightly, straining against biceps that looked more like softballs than tennis balls. I blinked away the thought of what lay beneath.

"Well, um, I hadn't really thought that far ahead. This was all kind of last minute, you know?"

He gave me that damn smile again, and a lock of black silk fell across one brow. I nearly fell over trying to stand. His hand steadied my arm before I realized what was happening. When he pulled me up, we were inches apart.

English became my second language. Hell, I forgot English existed.

"Wow, uh, thanks. I'm not…I mean, I don't usually…fuck."

He laughed, low and sexy. God, that sound fanned

the flame his touch had ignited. I tried to step back, to put space between us, but the damn wall was there. He stretched an arm out and placed a hand against the wall, leaning toward me.

I couldn't breathe. He smelled of musk and Irish Spring and General Tso.

Fuck you, General. Why did you have to be so damn spicy?

"You look tense. I have good hands, could give you a massage," he half whispered, half growled.

"Massage? Uh, what? Now? Really? I don't—"

*Oh. My. God.* Why had I turned into a thirteen-year-old girl about to get her first kiss? I'd fucked flight attendants into other time zones. Heath was just standing nearby and I was practically a puddle. *What the actual fuck?*

"Just a massage. Nobody's getting naked. We just met, after all."

I didn't trust my voice, so I nodded like the soon-to-be murder victim in a bad movie when the killer just asked him to go upstairs.

Heath smiled again. *Fuck.*

So, I did what any self-respecting idiot teen in a horror/thriller would do—I led him upstairs to my bedroom.

Jesse lay quietly at the foot of the bed, her fur tickling my toes, as Heath removed my shirt and pressed me gently down, face first.

"Close your eyes—and keep them closed. Just relax," he said.

Like that was going to happen. My heart was racing faster than a NASCAR driver on the final turn—or straightaway—or whatever NASCAR drivers did. What did I know?

The bed shifted as he stood and padded into the bathroom. I heard his footfalls accompanied by the squirty sound of a bottle shooting its goo into his hands. The bed shifted again, and I nearly leapt to the ceiling as cold lotion dripped between my shoulder blades. Heath barked out a low, rumbly laugh.

"Sorry, didn't realize it was that cold. I'll warm it up."

*I bet you will,* I thought as my heart tried to find its place in my chest once more.

And then his strong, steady hands began kneading my tight, chicken-shit-frightened shoulders and back. I forgot all about the cold sensation caused by the lavender lotion and let myself drift happily off into massage land. Damn, he knew how to use his hands.

He finished with my back and traveled up to my neck and shoulders where I carried most of my stress.

"Wow. Your neck is like a rock." His thumb dug into one side and I fought off a flinch.

"Yeah, welcome to my work."

"What do you do?"

"I'm an exec. for a financial company."

"Oh." Was that an eyebrow raise or snoozed reply? I couldn't tell. The meat of his palm pressed harder into my neck and I forgot to care.

When he finished rubbing my neck, I felt hot breath near my ear. "I need to warn you about something," he rasped.

"Huh?" was all I got out.

Two hundred pounds of muscle splayed against my back, pressing me into the bed. His cock twitched through his shorts, and my butt quivered.

"I make love like a wolf." His voice was thunder fucking lightning into submission.

Huh? My brain wouldn't function.

"I'm rough and powerful, and I growl when I like it—and I always like it." My dick was suddenly uncomfortable between our combined weight and the mattress.

"Oh." I was articulate as ever.

"But this is just a massage, so you don't need to worry."

"Uhh—"

Between his weight, his cock, and the idea of him fucking me like an angry wolf, words wouldn't form. Mental images of sex in the woods flashed through my head. I could hear his rumble, feel his breath, taste his—

He propped himself up, relieving my body of his weight. I wanted to reach back and pull him down again, but my arms wouldn't go that direction.

"Want to make out, just to see if there's a connection? I'd rather know up front if there's no chemistry."

I squirmed my way around to face him. His eyes strayed briefly down to my bare chest and abs, then back up. They brimmed with need.

"Yeah," I said. "Fuckin' kiss me."

Who the hell said that? Was that me or the devil?

*All you, Massage Boy. Enjoy.* The devil giggled.

Then the wolf pounced.

Lips locked. His tongue drove into my mouth and wrapped itself around my own. My breath was sucked out of me and I didn't care. Who the fuck needed to breathe when you could feel this good?

Holy shit, we fit together. His arms engulfed my whole body while his mouth devoured me. I tried to keep up, but he'd been honest. He was all wolf—all hunger and desire. It was passionate. No, it was primal.

Something in me began to panic, but he didn't stop. His weight pressed harder. He drove his cock down, and even through his shorts I felt its force against mine, and I wanted it.

My brain tossed the panic aside as I gave in to our lust. I gripped his arms, then his back, squeezing and clawing, pressing my fingers into the ridges of his deeply formed muscles.

God, his body was hard. There was no give when I pressed. It was like driving my thumbs into stone.

And that thought drove me crazier.

"Somebody's getting hard," he growled.

"God, yes."

His body trembled from a chuckle.

"Enough chemistry for you, Wolfy?"

He bit my neck, and I arched my back, pushing our dicks together and making him spasm.

"That's not fair," he protested.

"Fuck fair. Take your clothes off."

"Just a massage, remember?" he teased.

"Fucking take your clothes off and let the wolf off his leash. Now."

"So bossy." He pulled back, a wide, glimmering grin shining down. In one model-on-a-beach motion, he crossed his arms and whipped his shirt over his head, revealing chiseled pecs and rounded shoulders.

A thick pelt of perfectly sculpted hair blanketed his chest, then thinned into the most luscious trail of sexual deviance ever to lead one to a pot of gold.

*Fuck. Me.*

I realized I'd been staring, exploring every curve and line with my eyes, while he loomed above, fucking grinning. "Everything meet with your approval? Need another minute to look?"

"Asshole."

He chuckled.

I reached a hand out and traced the line of his chest, one finger delicately running through his hair. His skin burned, and I was sure I felt him tremble at my touch.

"Keep doing that and this massage is going to need a happy ending."

"This stopped being a massage the minute you kissed me." I was in the red zone. There would be no turning back. "Pants. Now. And kiss me more."

Fucking grin.

Then our lips met again. He kissed me while we both fumbled awkwardly with our shorts. He didn't take his underwear off, just pressed his full weight against me again. Now only two thin layers of cotton separated our most important of parts—and his wasn't that of a normal wolf. Oh no, this was a genuine *Game of Thrones* dire wolf dick, all big and hard and—

He flipped me over before I could finish reliving parts of those books I didn't think good ol' George actually wrote in them. His cock was now rock-hard and pressed against the crease of my underwear. He didn't have to position anything. It knew where to go. His hips slowly ground up and down, teasing my butt without separating it. I was puckered so hard he couldn't have driven in a needle with a sledgehammer, but I fucking wanted him to try. The more he rubbed and finally pressed, the more I wanted him inside me.

While his dick teased my ass, he dragged his teeth across my neck, nipping and taunting. He pinned my arms above my head with his hands, and sweat dripped from his burning body onto my back. I wanted him to douse me, drown me in that salty, musky moisture. When he pressed his chest against me, the slickness of his sweat met the coarseness of his hair. Thousands of pinpricks of pleasure and pain tickled my skin. I could feel every hair, all of them together, as his ridiculously ripped chest and abs scrubbed away my last inhibitions.

And then he pressed his cock into my crack. It had somehow come free of the flap in his briefs and drove deep, only the cloth of my own undies stopping it from going further. My body screamed with need as he drove harder and harder, dragged his body over mine, bit my lobes and licked my neck.

"I need you in me now."

His mouth pressed against my ear. "Beg me."

"Please. Fucking please. Take me any way you want. Just take me."

He bit my lobe again, this time harder. I twitched at the pain, then leaned into it.

His hands released my arms and dove into the waistband of my underwear. Rather than rip them off like I expected, he gripped my hips and squeezed my buttocks, exploring my now exposed skin like it was new territory for his map. Then his fingers wriggled their way in front and a fingertip found my head. He gently teased a drop of slickness, then pulled his fingers away. Everything he did made me want more.

His hands vanished and I felt his weight lift as he pulled his own underwear off, flinging it across the room with his feet. Then one hand found my abs and lifted me up while the other slowly dragged my underwear to my ankles.

He stilled for a long moment. "Wow."

I turned my head to look.

"Don't move," he said. "I want to memorize everything like it is right now."

It was my turn to grin. Granted, it wasn't his model-perfect, pearly white gleam—no, it was a goofy high-school-band-nerd-getting-a-kiss-from-a-cheer-leader grin—but it was a grin.

I lost track of how long his fingers gently traced every ridge of my legs, butt, back, and shoulders. The hungry wolf from moments earlier had retreated, replaced by a far more thoughtful, deliberate beast. I wanted so badly to ask what he was thinking, but his touch had the power to steal my voice. I couldn't speak or move—or think. All I wanted was to feel him —for him to never stop.

"Where's your lube?"

I could speak again. Just not English. "Uh, lube? Right. It's…um…I have it…bathroom. No…drawer. Yeah…in the side table."

*What the fuck?* I was a blithering idiot.

He chuckled. "You talk good."

His lips pressed into my neck before I could respond, stealing my voice once more.

I heard the drawer slide open, then the pop of the bottle.

Reality returned to my brain. I was an adult. I had to be an adult.

I sat up. "Heath, I'm positive."

I tried to keep my eyes on his, but their will was greater and they fell to my hands.

His meaty palm cupped my cheek and lifted them back to his. "So am I. If you want to stop, we can. Or we can use—"

I shook my head. "No."

He cocked his puppy dog head again.

"No, don't stop," I said, with more force than I'd intended. "And no, I don't want to use a condom… unless you want to. In that case, I'm okay with it."

*Michael Reed, what the hell are you doing?* The angel's voice boomed in my head. His invocation of the house on the opposite side of his neighborhood caught my attention. *You might already have HIV, but there are other strains. For heaven's sake, there are other diseases you could catch. You don't know this guy. You just met. For all you know, he's a human petri dish. Think before you poke. Please.*

*He's right, you know,* the devil said. Fuck, they agreed. *The smart thing to do is use protection. Better yet, don't have sex with strangers. But when have we done the smart thing? Remember Fly Boy?*

Why was Fly Boy always his go-to? Sheesh.

*Michael, this isn't a game. It's your life. It's his life too. Don't be stupid.* The angel was practically begging.

Then Heath's freshly lubed palm found my cock and both sides of my conscience faded into the distance. In the back of my mind, I knew I was being irresponsible. Hell, in the front of my mind I knew it. In that moment, though, my mind was no longer in control. We'd passed that point. Right or wrong, I would deal with the consequences later.

Heath had watched my internal dialogue, knowing I was struggling with an answer. Only when my eyes met his with firm resolve did his hand grip my dick, saturating it with oily heat and tender passion. I reached down and gripped him, once more giddy at the girth of his godlike groin. It was already dripping and slick.

His other hand found my hole. I jumped, startled, then tried to relax as he teased and tested, leaving a layer of lube just outside—and inside. Then his weight was on me again. His knees spread my legs apart, and I lifted them over his shoulders. His cock slid against my hole, and my body lurched.

Holy fuck, he was big.

He pressed, and the tip slid inside me. I clinched involuntarily, and he slipped out with a *pop*.

He did that head-cock thing again.

"Sorry, it's been a while. And you're kinda—"

He snickered. "Yeah, I'm big. I know. Just trust me."

He leaned down and kissed me, softly, full of passion. His lips drank me in. As his tongue caressed mine, he entered me again. Slowly, tenderly, his tongue pressed deeper. Our lips parted for air and I realized he was fully inside me. He pulled back slowly, then dove in once more, again and again. His fingers gripped my hair and pulled my head back into the pillow as his lips and teeth found my neck again. He'd leave a mark, but I didn't care. I needed him inside me.

As moments passed, tenderness became urgency. His posture rose, gaining leverage. His thrusts grew more forceful. Deliberate, methodical exploration devolved into desperate, driving passion. Grunts turned into growls, then groans. I freed my hands and gripped his butt, urging him deeper and harder. Faster. I wanted him so badly.

His breathing turned wild, and he leaned in. "If we keep doing this—"

"Shut up and fuck me."

He grabbed my wrists and slammed them against the pillows, then pulled my body toward him, thrusting him into me even deeper than before. Now fully on his knees, the wolf emerged to devour his prize. I heard myself growling and groaning in time to his thrusts and moans. Faster, harder, deeper. How could he go deeper? He gripped my hair again and howled at the ceiling. Drove himself with all his strength.

Our bodies shuddered together as he freed himself inside me. I'd not even touched myself, yet I painted his hairy stomach, whiteness smeared among the dark. He continued to thrust and shudder. My moans turned to whimpers, then his died completely. He collapsed onto my body, still inside me, trembling atop me.

A moment later, he kissed my neck.

"That was some massage," I said. "Sure glad nobody took their clothes off."

He shoved his semi-hard cock. "Very funny. You weren't complaining."

"Oh, I'm still not. You felt…amazing."

He beamed. "Really?"

Wow. In that blinding moment, I realized he had no idea how incredible he was.

"Heath, damn, you were rock-star level. And those kisses…"

"Yeah. You're pretty good yourself."

He kissed me again and my heart flipped.

As he sat up and pulled away, I heard him snort a laugh.

"What's funny?"

"Um. Party foul."

"What?"

"You got shit on my dick."

"Eww," I gasped. "Sorry, I really wasn't expecting to get fucked today, certainly not have a freight train shoved up my ass."

He snorted again as he walked into the bathroom to clean up. "Freight train. 'Choo choo,' says the Choco Train."

I fell back onto the bed and tried to hide the brilliant rouge flooding my face. He was waving his dick like it was rolling down a track, making *chugga-chugga* sounds.

Thanks a lot, Serena.

18

———

**BALLOON PARTY**

H eath came over for dinner the next night. I made roasted pork stuffed with goat cheese, cherries and nuts, glazed with a port wine and cherry reduction.

Don't get all hot and bothered. It was a recipe I'd found in a book about grilling meats. It sounded complicated and foo-foo, but was actually super easy to prepare. The trick was to get the cook right on the pork. A little under and, well, one might kill one's guest with raw pork. That would be a clear party foul. A little over, and the pork became dry and tough, losing all its sumptuous flavor. No amount of glaze or goat cheese could help a lifeless, gray piece of pork.

Jesse lay dutifully by his feet, staring up as he took his first bite. I stared from my chair opposite his at the table. He closed his eyes as he chewed, and I knew from the wet-dream look on his face I'd nailed the cook.

"Oh, Jeeeeesus. You never said you could cook like this," he muttered as his chewing slowed to a reverential crawl.

I grinned and shrugged. "It's just pork. Nothing special."

*You're such an ass. You know it's amazing,* the angel whispered with a slight giggle.

*Ass? Are you allowed to use big words like that?* the devil snarked.

*Fuck off. I can say a lot more than you might think. I just have to say it for the greater good.*

I took a bite of pork and all the voices vanished. Holy shit, Heath was right. This might've been the most delicious thing I'd ever cooked.

"Told ya." My eyes popped open to catch him grinning. "First bite? It really is fantastic."

I nodded and chewed, then moaned.

"I remember that sound." His grin grew wider.

I gave him a look that said, *Really? At the table while eating pork?*

Then my brain processed what I'd just thought, and I laughed out loud. He'd *porked* to get that moan. The irony was as thick as—

After dinner, we skipped the planned viewing of whatever reality show had caught our attention and raced each other upstairs, giggling like four-year-olds all the way. There were no careful caresses or slow massages. We tore off each other's clothes and had wild, mindless rabbit sex—you know, the kind where you mean to go all night, but bunnies were made in zero-point-three seconds flat?

"Uh, that was…um…quick." He sounded embarrassed.

I chuckled. My head was nuzzled on the bed of fur just beneath his chin. "Quick can be fun too. I don't think my butt could've handled thirty minutes of the USS Heath firing its long guns after what you did yesterday."

"USS Heath? You going all navy on me now?" His voice was playful.

"Sorry, you fucked my brain cells dry."

My head bobbed as his chest heaved with laughter. God, that felt good.

My mind spun.

*I will* not *like this guy. Absolutely not. I've given up on men, on dating—and most definitely on relationships. My heart can't take another bad ending. Hell, it hasn't even had a beginning in years. Nope, definitely not liking Heath. No way.*

As I lay there, I heard his heart beating. His deep, slow breaths mirrored my own. When he wrapped one arm around me and pulled me tighter into him, I thought I might die right there. When he kissed the top of my head and his other hand stroked my hair, I stopped thinking altogether. All I could do was close my eyes and sigh—and smile.

*Absolutely not. No, no, no. I refuse—*

It had been years since I'd felt so warm and safe, so *wanted.* I drank it in, savored it, willed the moment's tranquility throughout my mind and soul. We didn't know each other, and I knew it was silly to feel this way on a second date, but my brain wasn't functioning—and for once, my Gemini twins of a conscience remained blessedly silent.

In the safety and comfort of Heath's arms, enveloped by his warmth and soothed by the rise and fall of his chest, I drifted into a peaceful, dreamless sleep.

A HOT, WET TONGUE ROUSED ME. I BLINKED BLEARILY to find the sun rising and Jesse standing on the bed beside me, her nose centimeters from my own, her tongue lapping at my mouth.

"Yuck. Baby girl, do you mind *not* French kissing Daddy?"

A deep rumble to my right nearly startled me out of the bed. I looked over to find Heath propped up on one elbow staring at me. The annoyingly camera-ready fucker wore a shimmering smile, perfectly mussed hair with one curl begging for escape from its brethren, and nothing else. He lay on top of the covers in all his furry, naked glory. My eyes drifted down, and either he was happy to see me or mornings were a very good thing in his world. Hell, they were a good thing in mine now too.

"Morning, sleepy."

I smacked my disgusting morning-breath-laden lips and mumbled, "Morning."

He chuckled. A hand shot out and gently stroked my cheek. "You mumble when you sleep. I couldn't make out the words, but it sounded very serious."

My eyes widened. "Really?"

He nodded. "Yeah, it was cute. It took me a while to get sleepy, and I didn't want to move you. You were so peaceful laying there on my chest."

I didn't know what to say to that. Peaceful was *exactly* how it had felt.

"Uh, yeah, it was…nice, I guess."

He grunted. "You guess?"

"No, sorry, it *was* nice. I'm not a morning person. I need coffee."

I could feel his grin behind me as I rose and padded into the bathroom.

"Want to go get some?" he asked.

My head popped around the doorframe. "Huh? What?"

"Coffee. Want to go get some?" He shook his head and chuckled. "You really are out of it in the morning."

A weak smile and shrug later, I said, "Yeah. Always have been. And sure, let's go get something to eat and a caffeine IV, stat."

I showered and changed. Heath washed his face and threw on the clothes he'd worn the night before. They had that "recently used for fucking" look, but he didn't seem to care. I liked that.

Over coffee and the finest fare Denny's had to offer, Heath verbally daydreamed about the US Open. I could see him traveling to New York in his mind as he described the courts and players, the vendors and spectators. He was more passionate about tennis than anyone I'd ever known.

I took a bite of waffle and nodded like I understood. I was clueless.

"What's so special about the US Open?" I asked. "I mean, is it really that different from the French or the other majors?"

I may as well have slapped him.

"Seriously? Did you really just ask me that?"

I shrugged.

For the next twenty minutes, he described

attending the last three Opens, the up-close view of the practice courts, seeing Roger Federer walk out on Center Court (or whatever it's named—he called it by some old player's name I recognized but couldn't place).

Then he compared it to the French and Australian Opens, and Wimbledon. The Australian was too hot, held in the dead of the Down Under summer. He loved the French because the red clay slowed the ball, creating long points where twenty or thirty shots were common. Apparently, that was a good thing. Wimbledon was the only tournament he allowed to be somewhat on par with the US Open, giving the Brits credit for their traditions and flair. After all, any tournament with a Royal Box had to be special, he reasoned.

"Royal Box," I chuckled. "Sounds like some bad gay porn."

He gave me a syrupy grin. "You liked my Royal Box last night."

"All thirty-six seconds of it, sure."

"Oh, you're gonna pay for that," he growled.

"Promises, promises."

The conversation trailed off as he turned to slam his Grand Slam. Mid-bite, he looked up, chewed hard and swallowed, then asked, "You free Friday night?"

"Uh, sure. I think so. Why?"

"My best friend is throwing a birthday party at their hotel. Should be fun. I'd love you to be my date."

*Dammit. I'm* not *dating. No, no, no.*

"Sure, sounds great."

*Fuck.*

HEATH STAYED OVER WEDNESDAY NIGHT. I WAS actually sore and slightly bowlegged Thursday morning.

During the day, he trekked fifty minutes down to Sarasota where he coached gymnastics and all-star cheerleading. When I'd quizzed him about pom-poms, he swatted me and explained that all-star cheer was different from the poodle-skirted chant-callers I knew from basketball games. These were highly athletic, highly choreographed teams of girls and boys. They worked for endless hours perfecting their stunts and routines, then traveled, sometimes hundreds of miles, to compete against other teams. To Heath, all-star cheerleading was the perfect marriage of gymnastics, dance, and performance art.

I couldn't wipe the image of my muscular Heath and his pom-poms from my mind, but rolled with the explanation without protest. He promised to drag me to a competition sometime so I could experience the thrill of victory for myself. Something in the back of my mind warned against that course, but I couldn't help smiling at his enthusiasm. He was passionate about everything he did. It was endearing.

He stayed at the castle again Thursday night. We rationalized that since he didn't have to work in Sarasota on Friday, it would be easier to just go from my place to the party than to try to meet up sometime Friday afternoon—or to just meet at the party. Never mind that I had to work in the office on Friday. He could just hang out with Jesse for the day.

That's logical, right?

I was *not* dating. He was *not* living in my house, or moving in, or—damn it—*anything* that looked like a relationship. This was a good time where the guy happened to sleep over and let me lay my head on his chest while he held me and kissed my forehead.

That's *nothing* like dating. Absolutely nothing.

Fuck you and your snickering.

Friday evening, when Heath walked into the den wearing tight dark jeans and a tighter deep-burgundy shirt that hugged his arms and highlighted his eyes, I nearly stumbled as I strode out of the kitchen.

"This look okay?" he asked, glancing self-consciously down at his outfit.

"Oh, yeah, you look…really…I mean…great."

He beamed up. My knees wobbled when our eyes met.

"I'll take that."

*Shit.* Now all I could think about was one of us *taking* something the other had in abundance—and it wasn't smiles or good intentions.

"You almost ready?" he asked.

I looked down at my shorts and T-shirt and laughed awkwardly. "I need to get dressed. Give me ten minutes. Jesse can keep you company."

He sat on the couch and my traitorous pooch hopped up to snuggle beside him. She'd accepted him in the pack. That was almost as shocking as the first time I'd seen the anaconda beneath his undies.

Moments later, I descended the stairs in light blue jeans and a green collared shirt I'd found at a store in the mall marketing itself as the adult version of Abercrombie. It grated on me that I was too old for A&F, but life went on, I supposed.

A low whistle snapped my head up.

"You look like a present I need to unwrap." Heath rose to his feet and I could see through his jeans how much the rest of him was also rising. I giggled inwardly at the thought that *I* caused that. Pride warred with my PK awkwardness. Before I knew it, he was standing before me, cupping my cheek, kissing me deeply. I moaned at his tongue's touch.

"I missed you while you were upstairs. Please don't leave me like that again."

*I am not fucking dating. Besides, that's a terrible line. Absolutely stupid—*

"God, I missed—"

*Who said that?*

His mouth stopped whatever I was about to say. It stopped me from thinking too.

My eyes were closed when he pulled back. I felt his warm breath tickle my nose. He smelled of wintergreen mouthwash and sweet cologne. "We'd better get going. Teri's a ball of energy. Brace yourself."

His thumb brushed hair off my forehead. I still hadn't opened my eyes. His lips met mine for one last taste, tenderly this time.

I breathed out. "Okay. I'm good. I mean, we should go. Yeah, let's go."

Before turning away, he flicked the hair he'd just moved back onto my forehead. "Somebody needs to mess your hair up a little now and then. Leave that there."

I grinned. "Yes, sir."

---

HEATH HADN'T PREPARED ME FOR THE PARTY, OTHER than the one offhanded comment about Teri. We waltzed into Teri's family hotel, a historic building in the heart of Ybor City. Everything in the place was original; period pieces and art dating back a hundred years or more. A smattering of twenty and thirtysome-things dressed in their best night-on-the-town outfits stood in groups of twos and threes.

We'd made it halfway across the elegant lobby before—

"Heeeeeeeeathy-poo!" a woman's voice squealed.

Before I could register a snappy retort to my new favorite nickname that would haunt Heath as long as we knew each other, a tall, thin woman with dark hair that fell to her butt raced across the room and nearly knocked Heath to the ground with her hug. I took an involuntary step back and watched the collision—and Heath's ensuing discomfort—with sadistic pleasure.

"Hey, Teri-poo," Heath said as he nuzzled her neck with his nose and kissed her cheek. When he surfaced, they shared a wide smile, staring at each other a moment. Then he remembered he wasn't alone and pulled back.

"Teri, this is Michael."

She turned to me and, without a second of hesita-tion, barreled into me just as she had Heath. The only thing that saved me was her lack of space to gather speed. Two strides did not a runway make.

"Hi, Mikey," she said, calling me my least favorite

variation of my name. I received the same peck on the cheek, but did not offer her the requisite neck nuzzle.

In a blur, she untangled our arms, pecked Heath again, and sped on to her next victims.

"That was a Teri drive-by. You may want to call your insurance," Heath said with a wide smile.

"I guess you warned me."

"Oh, that was calm Teri. Just wait."

"Awesome."

Heath reached over and dusted the makeup off my shoulder. He called the lipstick or makeup left in Teri's wake "Teri droppings." It seemed appropriate.

"Let's go downstairs. The others should be here by now. I want you to meet my friends."

*Meeting friends is a dating thing, isn't it? Something I clearly am not supposed to be doing. Nor getting nose-nuzzled.*

"Sounds great," I said as he took my hand, interlaced our fingers, and pulled me like a puppy on his first leash.

*Nor interlacing fingers. What bedeviling fuckery is at play here?*

We wound our way around an antique staircase you might see in an ancient library, the kind that winds in a circle so many times you're dizzy by the time your foot steps on the floor below. I thought the wrought iron was cool until the room started spinning.

Heath never let go. He never unlocked…de-laced…unlaced…pulled our fingers apart. Whatever. I was screwed.

The first thing I realized as my feet touched down was the lighting in the party room was several lumens lower than in the lobby, giving the place a swanky vibe that fit perfectly with all the antique furniture and their velvety coverings. A trio played jazzy music in the corner as servers in red vests and black ties roamed throughout the small crowd with appetizers on silver trays.

"Heath!" virtually every voice in the room called as my non-date appeared. Guys strode over to clap him on the back or give him a sturdy hug. Women pecked his cheeks and squeezed his biceps appreciatively.

Something odd bubbled in my chest at that. Why did I suddenly dislike those women?

*Weird.*

"Come over here. Look, they're taking pictures."

In the corner was a wall of red balloons pinned to a shiny green backdrop. It looked like Christmas and Valentine's Day had mated and their baby was a photo booth. Heath pulled our still-interlaced hands and positioned us dead center.

"Can you take several? I want to pick the best one. Okay?" Heath seemed really excited about these pictures. I'd always hated having mine taken, was self-conscious of how the camera washed out my pasty skin. Being the awkward kid never fully left a person. On that night, I didn't have a choice. There was no running from that camera.

*Flash. Flash, flash. Pop, flash, flash.*

I blinked. The room was filled with dots.

"That's perfect. I love it," Heath said, examining the screen on the photographer's camera. "Can you email those to me?"

A moment later, the dots had cleared and Heath was showing me our pictures.

*Our* pictures. Our *first* pictures.

On the screen, Heath stood on the left. His teeth reflected the flash like a freakin' mirror. They were stills, but his hair somehow flowed. His skin practically glowed. How could anyone be that photogenic?

The washed-out guy next to him had a decent smile. One errant curl of reddish hair bobbed on his forehead.

"You look so cute there." Heath squeezed my shoulders and kissed my head.

"You look like you just stepped off a photo shoot. How do you do that?"

"What?" His smile was so wide it *had* to hurt.

"Always look good in pictures? Every pic you've ever taken on Facebook is model-perfect, even the candid ones and selfies—especially the candid ones. There should be a law against being that good in front of a camera."

He kissed me again. "It's a curse. Hope you're okay with it."

I snorted. "I guess. Any other tragic flaws I need to be aware of?"

"Plenty, but no cheating. You'll have to learn those on your own." His head snapped up and he called out, "Karl!"

Then he bounded across the room to be enveloped in the arms of a giant. I'd thought Heath tall at six foot two, but this dude had to stand six seven, maybe six eight, and he was thick and muscular, not skinny like some really tall guys. With Heath in the way, all I saw were massively thick arms and a losing battle over thinning hair. When Karl looked up, I realized the follicle fight didn't matter. His face was striking with or without a fancy 'do.

"Babe, come here." Heath motioned me over.

*Aww. He just called you babe,* the devil mocked.

I froze. *Shit.* He was right, he had called me babe. Was that allowed? You know, for guys who were definitely not dating?

*You're* so *dating. Just admit it. You want more than just his dick, don't ya?* The devil was relentless.

*Hey, angel, a little help over here*, I silently pleaded.

*Not a chance. For better or worse, he's right. You let your ass do the talking, and this is what you get. Good luck.*

"Come on. This is Karl." I'd been too lost in thought to see Heath approach and grab my hand again, pulling me over to stand before the Giant of Judgment. Shit, he was tall—and hot. I gaped up. My mouth wouldn't work.

"Nice to meet you, Michael. Heath's told us good things." The giant extended a hand. My own disappeared into his palm as he squeezed the life out of my knuckles. I don't even think he was trying to squeeze. His natural strength level was set to maximum, and he didn't know any lower. I gritted my teeth in a painful approximation of a smile while pretending not to be dying inside. My poor hand.

When I turned to Heath for help, he'd vanished.

"He's gone to check on Teri," Karl said. "He usually helps her get set for parties like this."

"Okay." I didn't know how to respond to that. Were parties a common thing? I thought this was her birthday—or the giant's—I couldn't remember. And what was there to set up? I looked around the room and hotel workers had done all the setup I could see. I shrugged it off and made small talk with the big man.

Ten minutes later, Teri and Heath reappeared. She talked a thousand words a minute and bounced from one group of friends to the next. When she settled by my side, she practically melted into Karl's body. Their kiss was so intimate I felt like I was intruding by watching. That kiss offered the only breath in her otherwise unpunctuated, Charles Dickens-esque dialogue. She spoke so quickly I could barely keep up.

Then Heath spoke and he matched her energy. He babbled incessantly while she prattled on, neither bothered that the other spoke at the same time. I watched them carry on two separate conversations aimed at the other, and I swear they knew exactly what the other was saying. It was dizzying.

I looked up to find Karl grinning down at me. "They're a lot, especially together. Let's get you a drink."

We left the party around one o'clock in the morning. The hotel sat on the edge of Ybor, making it an easy walk to the party district of Tampa. Most of the guests were headed down the street to continue their celebrations. Heath said he usually went with them, especially if Teri and Karl were leading the charge, but that night he just wanted to take me home and do nasty things together.

He rubbed my leg all the way home. It wasn't the gentle fingertip stroking I'd come to know. It was the firm, hungry rubbing of a man who wanted to strip naked the moment the door slammed shut.

So we did.

That night, in two rounds of reckless, passionate, animalistic sex, Heath fucked me so hard I thought my uterus might fall out—and I don't even have one of those puppies.

I didn't know what had gotten into him, but I liked it. Fuck, I loved it.

He threw me onto the bed and spread my legs apart like he owned them, like he owned every part of me. There was no foreplay, no lovey-touchy-kissy lead in. He grabbed the lube, doused us both, then dove into me. I'd never been driven so hard or fast— or hard. Did I say hard? *Fuck.*

As we neared the end of round two, Heath was up on his knees with my ankles tossed over his shoulders. I swear he had a leg up my ass all the way to his knee, and he was shoving with all his might. That's when we heard it.

A loud *crack.*

Heath froze mid-thrust. His eyes were wild and wide. Mine were bleary.

Another *crack,* this one louder.

Then the bed fell and Heath tumbled out of me and over the side.

I hopped up, now fully alert. "Heath! Are you okay? Holy crap. Talk to me."

It started as a low rumble, then grew to a roar. Before I knew it, Heath was laughing hysterically. He pointed. My eyes followed his finger. His laughter redoubled, then mine joined his. Tears were streaming down our cheeks as we lay on that floor howling.

The mattress lay askew. The wooden railing that held it was no longer visible; only shards.

We'd broken the bed.

# DRAWERS

I didn't see Heath for a couple days. No, it wasn't because of the bed. He had to go see his mom in Alabama. Something was going on with his sister, and his mom needed help. It was odd. He hadn't held back with any other subject, but his family was a sore point. He seemed almost, I don't know…ashamed. It was weird. I didn't press, just told him to have a good trip and drive safely.

On the first day of his trip, I went to a local furniture store and picked a replacement for my utterly destroyed bed frame. I couldn't help the chuckle as I strolled through the showroom with a most helpful sales lady, who asked what was most important to me in my new bed.

"Durability," I said through laughter she couldn't understand. I think she expected an explanation, but there was no way I was giving her one. She'd just have to speculate.

In the end, I chose a very sturdy mahogany frame with six built-in drawers fitted neatly under the mattress. My house was historic, but its closet and drawer space were historically lacking. Plus, if Heath wanted to continue sleeping over, I thought it might be nice to have a place for his underwear and things.

*You're so dating,* the angel quipped.

*Yep. Gotta agree with Glowy over there. You're whipped—and not just up the ass like—*

"Thanks, guys. I got it. No mental image needed."

*You broke a bed. Your mental image is very physical—and in pieces.* The devil howled with laughter as he vanished.

The angel actually patted my cheek in pity. That was a new low.

On the second day of Heath's trip, I sat on my sectional on one end of the L while Jesse sprawled out on the other piece. She glared at me like I'd done something to scare her new bestie away.

"He's gone to see his mom. I promise I didn't disappear him like in the movies. He'll be back soon."

She looked away, unconvinced.

I stared at the television. And, for the first time, realized I missed him.

## 20

ALABAMA

Heath came straight from Alabama to my place. I'd rehearsed his return in my head. There would be no running from across the room into his arms. No, I would not do the fawning, "I missed you" thing. Never mind that I *had* missed him. I wasn't supposed to be dating, and a single guy didn't miss another single guy he wasn't interested in.

The moment the door handle wiggled, I was off the couch, running to the door, and buried myself in his chest and arms.

"Woah," he laughed as he set his bag down and raised his arms to hug me. "Can a guy get in the door before he's expected to perform? Sheesh."

I pulled back and punched his chest. "Dork."

He pulled me back into him and kissed me deeply. "I missed you too."

I fucking melted. *Dammit.*

He lifted his duffel over his shoulder, and I led him upstairs.

"So," I said over my shoulder as we ascended. "I have a surprise, but don't read too much into this. My rule stands."

"Rule? You have a rule?" He smacked my butt.

"Not about sex. You broke all those. No moving in before a year of dating. That's always been my rule."

Okay, yes, most observant reader, I shattered that with Ryan. Stop judging.

"Oh, I don't want to move into this shabby place," he teased. I knew he loved the castle. Then he stepped into the bedroom and whistled. "Now that's a bed. We'll have to work extra hard to break that puppy."

I barked a laugh. "I'm afraid I'll be in more pieces than the bed if you break this one. It's built like a tank."

He wiggled his bushy black brows. "Have you met the USS Heath? It's a battleship. Ships beat tanks."

I rolled my eyes and laughed, then pointed down below the mattress. "Those two are for you."

His eyes followed my finger, then those bushy brows slowly rose. "My own drawers? So I won't move in?"

"Shut up," I said in my most mature voice.

He tossed his duffel on the floor and grabbed me

roughly. "I've never wanted to break a bed more than I do right now. Fuck the drawers."

We were naked before I had time to show him the headboard's mini-drawer and its new pump-action bottle of lube. The fucker found it without any help.

---

"HOW'S YOUR MOM?" I ASKED WHILE TRAILING MY fingers through his sweaty, lube-slicked chest hair.

Yes, he had lube up there. Don't ask questions.

He grunted. "She's okay. She wants to move down here."

I waited for him to explain. When he didn't, I asked, "That's a good thing, isn't it? You'd be closer to each other."

He grunted again. "Yeah, we'd be closer."

This time I just waited. I thought he'd fallen asleep, but he finally spoke again, this time in a quiet, pensive voice. "I didn't have the same childhood as… well, anybody else. I don't even know my dad. I think I know who he is—which one he is, I mean. My mom was very…popular."

I didn't know what to say to that. My childhood could've been on an episode of *Leave It to Beaver* or *The Andy Griffith Show*. I knew other families weren't

always like ours, but I had no idea some were so irrev-
ocably broken.

"My mom was drunk a lot when I was younger. I'd find her in the hallway passed out, half naked, sometimes totally naked." He thought a moment. "I was six, maybe seven, the first time I found her naked and had to help her into bed. I remember eating Froot Loops at the table with some man the next morning. He hadn't been in her bed when I put her there, but he ate breakfast with me. He wore a uniform and had a gun. I think he was some kind of cop. I never got his name."

I sat up and leaned on my elbow and watched his eyes drift further into the past. My hand never left his chest.

"My brother was murdered when he was a teenager. He was a really bad guy, ran with a lot worse, but nobody deserves to be murdered. Cops thought some drug gang executed him." He shifted onto his side and looked up. His eyes pleaded. I wasn't sure for what. My heart ached for him. "My sister tried to kill my mom."

"What?" I was stunned.

He nodded slowly. "Stabbed her a dozen times through the covers while she lay in bed. Docs couldn't believe Mom even made it to the hospital alive, but she proved them all wrong and lived through it. My sister's been in jail ever since—but she's getting out. That's why I went home."

What could I even say to any of that? This poor man.

"My mom wants to move here so my sister doesn't know where she is. She's scared."

"I bet she is."

He looked up, tears brimming in his eyes. "But you don't know my mom. She's a sweet little old lady, but she's manipulative. If she comes here, she'll try—"

"She'll try what?"

He shook his head. "I'm sorry. You don't want to know all that. It's terrible enough I have to know it."

I cupped his cheek, turning his eyes back to mine. "Heath, listen to me. I'm here, and I'm not going anywhere. I wasn't planning on dating. Hell, I was trying to avoid it. But what I feel for you—"

He smiled for the first time in long moments. "I feel it too."

"You shattered my no dating rule. Then you broke my bed. Now you're moving shit into drawers. Heath Cox, you're going to be the end of me, aren't you?"

He gripped my head in both of his strong, meaty palms. "Only if I'm lucky."

I lost myself in the kiss that followed.

That's when I stopped fighting it—the idea of

dating or relationships or whatever. I stopped fighting the idea that I could be happy again. Or hurt again. I stopped fighting Heath and his ridiculous smile and maddening, knee-weakening eyes.

My heart had known long before my head caught up.

It had only been a few weeks since Serena beat Azarenka—and yes, every part of that sounds ridiculous when I say it out loud—but I knew we'd find a way.

**21**

_________

## DO YOU LIKE YOUR BALLS HARD
## OR YELLOW?

The following Saturday marked the beginning of the fall softball season. Tampa, being a wonderfully tropical Florida enclave, enjoyed warm weather most months of the year, affording us the opportunity for outdoor sports leagues when other cities were huddled about fireplaces roasting weenies —or whatever miserable people up north did. I was thankful not to know the right answer to that question.

Heath surprised me by offering to come play with me. He'd never played softball on a team, but was extremely athletic and confident in his ability to master any sport he tried. I loved the idea of playing on teams together, as it would let us bond within a shared circle of friends while spending more time together.

We warmed up and our coach came over to watch

and evaluate. Heath was a beast with a bat. His first few swings launched the ball twenty yards over the fence. I thought our coach was going to run out onto the field and hug him. He later told me the mechanics of batting felt a lot like the snap of a forehand in tennis. It just made sense to him. Once he mastered the timing, balls flew. It was a thing of beauty.

Satisfied with his offensive skills, we switched to defense. He picked up the hand–eye coordination required to catch almost immediately. Coach had him field fly balls in the outfield, and he ran down everything they hit at him. When moved to the fast-paced infield, he did even better. Years of swatting at tennis balls had taught him to follow the line of the ball better than most guys on the team. The buzz about our new player was beginning to build.

And then he threw the ball.

Let's not be generous—his throwing was *beyond* terrible. He had a clinically diagnosable case of throwing dyslexia, perhaps the worst case ever seen. It was chronic. There was no treatment. He would not recover.

Old friends from Atlanta introduced me to that term, explaining it occurred when a softball player tried to throw the ball in one direction, but it consistently chose its own path. Poor Heath. I tried helping him. The coach tried. Half the team tried. It was useless. His tosses went sideways or backward or, worse, straight down into the dirt. Any time he caught a ball and had to throw to a baseman during a drill, the entire infield cringed; some ducked instinctively. No one knew where his toss would go, least of all him.

For a stud of state-championship athletic proportions, he was dreadful.

We were a C-level team, meaning most of the players knew which end of the bat to use, but we weren't highly skilled. Heath's hiccups with throwing fit in well with our Bad News Bears fielders and batters. In fact, his incredible skill in those two areas balanced out some of our weaknesses. Coach decided to play him at first base, where he would catch far more than throw. It just made sense. As we neared the end of our first practice together, the future was looking bright for our softball season…

Until coach put Heath back in the outfield for more fly ball practice and my dummy non-boyfriend dove for a foul ball. Who dives for a foul ball in practice? Let the ball drop. He didn't know that little unwritten rule of laziness in adult sport. He dove… and dislocated his shoulder.

I raced him to the hospital, where a spindly-looking doctor who mustered more strength than I thought he possessed snapped everything back into place. Heath's writhing ceased immediately.

In the car on the way back to the castle, he turned to me. "I really liked softball today. You know, until—"

I didn't mean to chuckle, but he was poking fun at himself. "You're supposed to let fouls drop during practice."

"Now he tells me."

I rolled my eyes.

"Maybe I should stick to tennis. Would you ever want to learn a new sport?"

That gave me pause. *Huh. Tennis.* I'd never played, other than smacking balls over the fence a few times. I was pretty sure that wasn't the goal, but it had felt good at the time, like a home run in every other sport that mattered.

On a whim, I said, "Sure. Sounds fun. Know anyone who can teach me?"

He grinned.

I knew that grin. I was so screwed.

<hr>

HEATH TOOK ME TO HIT A FEW DAYS LATER. HE scowled at my racket. It was the same aluminum-framed beast I'd used when I tried out for my high school team. All the other kids had started playing when they were three, while I was walking onto the court for my first time thinking, "This will be easy."

It was *not* easy. I did not make the team.

We started near the net with something he called "mini-tennis." It felt weird standing only a few feet away, trying to keep the ball just over the net, but he swore it was one of the best drills to get a feel for the ball. We eventually stepped back to the baseline and tried to rally. Heath was amazing, and not just because his hair bounced as he moved. At nearly forty years old, he still played at a small college level. I was lucky just to track the ball, much less hit it. More of my strokes smacked the back fence than the court. After ten minutes of futile feeding, he motioned me up to the net.

"So, I think we may need to start with different lessons."

I hated being bad at anything. Damn it, I was athletic. This shouldn't be so hard.

"Don't beat yourself up. Tennis is one of the hardest sports. People don't think that, but it is, and everything is up to you. There's no team to help you or have your back. You did fine for your first time, but we need to spend more time doing footwork and basic drills before you're ready to rally—at least, until we get your level up to…well, just up."

I liked him wanting to help me get it up, then I

realized he was talking about my tennis level. The boner that was starting to form deflated.

"Okay. Put me in, coach."

"Wrong sport, but I'll take it." He chuckled and shook his head. "We'll need a basket of balls and a hopper."

"Hopper?"

"It's a wire basket with a long handle to help pick up balls. You'll see."

He spent the next thirty minutes teaching me basic feeding and footwork drills, hitting patterns, and how to properly toss for a serve.

Yes, there is a proper way to toss a tennis ball.

These drills became part of our routine. I went to the office. Heath drove to Sarasota. We'd meet afterward on a tennis court and drill, followed by dinner at the castle—which I cooked because he was a terrible cook and I dreamed of becoming a chef. We ate on the couch while Jesse stared intently from the other end of the sectional. Her head would rise like a telescope when she'd hear Heath's fork land on his plate the final time. How she knew it was the final time was a mystery. She just knew.

Yes, we let her lick the plates. Neither of us could refuse my baby girl.

While Jesse hoovered the glazing off the porcelain, we'd flip through channels, usually landing on

*American Idol*, *Survivor*, or some random match on the Tennis Channel. It didn't matter who was on, Heath clung to every stroke.

Of the tennis matches…*tennis* strokes. Stop being dirty!

Then we'd get naked and other strokes took over. *Now* you can be dirty.

He never again slept in the bedroom he rented from an older married couple across town. Five months after Serena, we drove to the house and retrieved the last of his things.

He ended up using *all* the drawers in the new bed.

Most nights, I fell asleep on his chest, reveling in his steady breath and beautiful warmth.

Most mornings, I woke to his fingers tracing my back or shoulder, or his lips kissing my neck as Jesse tickled my toes with her devilish tongue. She would not be out-loved by some man—not even the man she'd fallen for the moment he'd walked through our door and fell to the ground to greet her before acknowledging my existence.

What can I say? My baby girl has good judgment.

**22**

---

## FOIE GRAS

Heath introduced me to the joys of the GLTA—
the Gay and Lesbian Tennis League, a world
tour of local organizations and tournaments in more
than seventy cities around the globe. Florida boasted
four of these tournaments: the Citrus Classic in
Tampa, the Orange Blossom in Orlando, the Art Deco
in Miami, and the Clay Court Classic in Fort Lauderdale. There was even a tournament where each of
these four key cities competed against each other
team-tennis style, called the Florida Cup.

Heath was already a member of Advantage Tampa
Bay, our local club. After a quick investment in a new
racket, bringing my equipment out of the Dark Ages,
we signed me up as a member of ATB so I could
participate in local league play. Heath was determined

I get as much match play as possible, arguing it was the only way to "learn to win."

Who was I to argue? He wasn't just a stud. He was a tennis stud.

Did I mention how watching him play made me weak at the knees? Fuck. How could a big guy like that move so well? While he got to almost every ball, Heath didn't look fast on the court. I nicknamed him Turtle, which he absolutely hated. Once I learned how much he hated it, I did the only thing a respectable boyfriend could do—I ordered a turtle vibration dampener for his racket.

Magically, that nickname became his favorite. I overheard him bragging about his turtle dampener on more than one occasion before a match. It made me giggle.

Nine months after we met, the baby came.

Stop that! Of course there was no actual baby. We're dudes—and my uterus fell out chapters ago. Keep up here.

Fourteen months post-Serena, we played in our first GLTA tournament together, the local Tampa Bay Citrus Classic, played on the Har-Tru green clay of the Harbor Island Athletic Club. Heath entered in the A division, the second highest, while I competed with the other rookies in D.

Heath won two rounds, but was defeated by an arch-nemesis from Fort Lauderdale in the third round.

I won my first trophy, besting the seven others in the Bad News Bears division.

Heath cried when they presented me the blown-glass orange with "Champion" emblazoned on the metal tag. I still remember the look in his eyes as I walked off that court. No man—not even Ryan—had looked at me with such pride.

I promptly tripped over the raised lip of the sideline and gasped as the sacred orange rolled across the clay to rest at his feet, thankfully unbroken. The queens around him roared with laughter, and we joined them as soon as he helped me up and dutifully dusted the clay off my knees and shorts. His hand lifting me from my fall sent tremors through my heart. There's nothing like knowing someone is there to pick you up when you fall to make butterflies dance. Why is that?

A few guys let out "Aww" at his display.

I didn't trust myself to speak after he kissed me in front of them.

I suppose the Citrus Classic was our first true coming out as a couple. Heath was well known in the gay tennis community, but they'd never seen him with a serious boyfriend. I lost track of the guys who whispered, "Good for you," or "Finally, someone got him."

We left Harbor Island exhausted, and I think there was clay lodged in places it didn't belong, but we held each other's hands as we walked to the car, only letting go long enough to hop in and buckle up. I was a reigning champion for the first time, and he was just the most beautiful man alive. There's a trophy for that, isn't there?

We played three more tournaments over the following six months. I didn't win anymore trophies. Neither did he. We did, however, receive the same "Awws" and "Good for yous" in every city we visited.

Those were better than any damn orange.

---

THE SECOND ANNIVERSARY OF SERENA ROLLED around. We celebrated with a trip to the US Open in New York. Our girl was there, whipping every ass she encountered.

Not literally. On the court. Serena's a lady.

You behave.

When we arrived at LaGuardia Airport to return home, Heath grabbed my hand and pulled me away from the security line.

"What's up, babe? You okay?" I asked.

"So, I kind of did a thing."

My brows rose.

"You have the next week off from work."

"What?" I was dumbfounded. "How—"

"I talked to your work son, who talked to your boss, who talked to HR. You have the week off. They're not letting you back in the building."

I wasn't sure I liked him tinkering with work. That could go in all sorts of bad directions—and would impact us both—but I let him keep going. Something was seriously up if they'd agreed to his mysterious plan.

"We're not flying home from here," he said tentatively.

"Uh-huh."

"Look, I'm no good with words on the spot. You know that. Take this." I glanced down at the boarding pass in his hand. The airport code wasn't one I recognized upside down. I took it and held it up.

It was a flight from New York to Paris.

My eyes snapped up to his. He was positively beaming.

"You…we're…we're going to Paris?"

"Happy anniversary, babe."

"You're taking me to Paris?" It still wasn't registering. My body was numb. Heath didn't make a ton of money as a coach. This would've set him back months of salary, maybe half a year. My eyes traveled from his face to the ticket then back up. They were losing a battle with an approaching tsunami, and he knew it. That fucker.

"Heath Cox. What am I going to do with you?" I stood there, in the middle of the bustling airport, surrounded by hustling passengers, with tears rolling down my cheeks.

"Kiss him!" a woman in a small crowd I hadn't seen gather yelled out.

"Go on. Give him a wet one," another yelled.

We both laughed, then I threw my arms around him and kissed him as deeply as I ever had. With the exception of our applauding peanut gallery, the rest of the traveling public ignored us. They had flights to catch. Then I remembered the time printed on the boarding pass. So did we.

PARIS WAS EVERYTHING I'D EVER DREAMED IT WOULD be. Napoleon's design was stunning. The people were fashionable—and friendly, no matter what anyone says. The Parisians we met were warm and kind. They appreciated that I tried to remember French from college, but quickly switched to English before I could permanently mar their unparalleled tongue.

I suppose they were right to do that. My French was awful.

Oh, but Heath's was worse.

On our first day, he tried to order for himself at a breakfast restaurant. The server spoke perfect English, but Mr. Confident Turtle wanted to impress me. He gave his order. The server quirked a brow, then repeated it with a very large question mark. Heath nodded emphatically, pointing at the menu. The server, now befuddled, turned to me.

"Monsieur veut des escargots pour le petit déjeuner? Vraiment?"

I spit my coffee and doubled over. The waiter joined me.

Heath crossed his arms. "What's so funny?" he demanded.

"What did you order?" I asked. He had to tell me. Even the waiter hung on his next words.

"Well—" He no longer sounded so confident. "I ordered eggs and ham on some kind of bun or bread, maybe a muffin. I couldn't get that word."

The waiter and I exchanged a look and cracked up again.

"What?" Now he sounded wounded.

"Babe, you ordered snails—for breakfast. You were looking at the dinner menu."

His face fell as he stared down at the menu.

The waiter and I wiped tears away, and I ordered for us both. From the kitchen, I could hear the waiter's excited voice replaying the scene. The roar of laughter told us the server would get miles out of the episode.

Our hotel sat diagonally across from the Louvre. We could walk to so much: shops, the Arc de Triomphe, restaurants, art galleries, you name it.

Notre Dame had yet to burn, and we marveled at the detailed splendor of its carvings. Neither of us was particularly religious—yes, I know, ironic for the PK —but there was no denying the majesty of France's most famous cathedral. For those who never saw the place before its tragic fire, you missed something special.

We visited everything from palaces to parade grounds. The Eiffel Tower had only recently begun lighting up at night, and we were both amazed when the glittering began. We were among the many couples holding hands and kissing in the lights beneath a full moon.

As beautiful as everything was, my eyes always found a way back to his. There was no sight in Paris to rival his chocolaty orbs. I could've skipped the tours and lost myself in his gaze forever.

What am I saying? We were in *Paris*. I needed to see everything. There would be plenty of time for eye-gazing after the day's activities.

Heath had it all planned out. He knew I loved to make the most of a trip and would want to see every sight we could cram in, but he also managed to schedule some downtime.

On our last night in Paris, we ate at an outdoor café. The air was crisp, and we were both bundled in our most fashionable coats and scarves. Like most cafés, the tables faced outward so diners could observe the streets. Heath and I sat side by side and people-watched as we ate. Our hands parted to take a bite or cut something, then found their way back together without word or command. We were alive in the most enchanting city either of us had ever visited, and we breathed in its magic as though life itself was at stake.

Heath stared out at the passing tourists. I couldn't stop watching him. His eyes positively glowed in the gas lamplight of the restaurant's façade. He wore a silly beanie he knew I hated, more to poke at me than to stay warm. His lips were parted in a slight smile that never quite left his lips.

Maybe that's what struck me most. His beautiful smile never faded—not when we were together.

As he gazed outward and I turned to avoid being caught staring, a man walked by. He was slim, but athletic. I could see that through his tight-fitting shirt, which was an oddity since it was chilly. He wasn't wearing a coat.

Now curious, I watched him more closely.

There was something familiar. The slight curl to his deep brown, almost black hair. His confident gait. I couldn't place what felt so recognizable—until he turned and glanced at our table.

It was his eyes. I could've sworn they belonged to—

No, that's ridiculous. Joseph would've been nearly fifty. The guy walking by didn't look a day over… well, shit. It could've been him.

Joseph. My first.

The guy vanished into the night, leaving my mind drifting wistfully into the past. I watched my younger self walk into Joseph's antique-filled apartment. I could smell the leather of his high-backed throne, see his wall of movies.

A smile tugged at the corner of my mouth, and I barely suppressed a chuckle as the image of Stephen Baldwin sandwiched between a guy and a gal popped into my head.

I'd been such a dork. How could any human being have been that clueless? Seriously?

Despite supreme naivete, that night had opened so many doors, doors I never even knew existed. I'd been so innocent and wide-eyed, so afraid to consider who I might be, or might become.

That night taught me to question. I learned that sometimes answers affirm our beliefs. Others force us to challenge and discard them. *Discard* may be a poor choice of word. *Respectfully disagree* might be more appropriate. However it should be defined, one thing was certain. That night with my roommate's friend changed the course of my life. It changed what I knew, and what I *thought* I knew. It changed how I saw others, and what I sought in them.

I didn't know it at the time, but that night changed *everything.*

The memories were so vivid and present in my mind's eye, yet it felt like a lifetime ago.

"Babe, where'd you go?" Heath said, as he squeezed my hand and nudged my shoulder affectionately.

Startled out of the recollection, my head turned toward him. His gaze was strong and pure. There were only possibilities in his eyes, opportunities and chances he wanted to take with me, a *lifetime* of them. In that frozen moment, bundled against a chilly, clear Parisian night, my heart finally and fully opened to a beautiful, boundless life of laughter and love.

So many times I thought I'd known *forever*. So many times I'd been wrong.

That night, beyond reason or doubt, I knew Heath was my forever.

He was my last date.

# EPILOGUE

D earest reader,
 We need to talk.

It's not usual for an author to address a reader directly. In fact, it's viewed by some in the literary community as a shattering of norms and rules that should guide all texts of quality. While I understand the style in which I wrote may seem unusual or awkward to some, the singular goal was to present a fun, honest story in a new and personal way.

Therefore, to those who cried foul at this attempt at innovation, I wish you well as you read other works. Every book isn't for every reader. I'm good with that. We're still friends. Sort of.

To everyone else—yes, I'm talking to *you*—thank you for sticking with me on this journey. Your emails, reviews, and DMs were filled with amazing comments and suggestions that never failed to lift my spirit. *You* are the reason I write, and hearing how much you love my characters or enjoy my stories makes my heart full.

Curiosity is a terrible beast when left unfed. So, before we wrap things up, I would like to address a few comments and answer questions raised throughout the writing of this series.

---

*Is this really a true story?* I get this one a lot. Yes, sir or ma'am, this series really is a true story. I changed names, locations, and altered some timelines, but the guts of the tale are indeed my real-life adventure. Yes, the foam party *really* happened—exactly as it was described. It was the single hottest sexual experience of my life (to date). One day, I'll recover. I doubt those who watched ever will.

Some authors advised me not to reveal the autobiographical nature of this series, but I thought you should know. I *wanted* you to know. I wanted to have an open, honest dialogue with readers by telling my own story in my own snarky voice.

---

*WERE YOU REALLY THAT CLUELESS? SURELY NOT. NO one is that clueless.* Au contraire, mon frère, I was indeed that lost little lamb who'd been sheltered from the world and all its bountiful gayness. My childhood was in the '70s and '80s. It was a different time. And yes, my dad really was a part-time preacher for fifty-six years. *Sheltered* barely defines what I was.

---

*IN THE FIRST BOOK, WHY WASN'T YOUR SATURN TOTALED when you had that accident?* Well, ask the insurance company that one. I'd had the car a month when I wrapped it around that tree. They saw fit to pay a ridiculous amount to have it repaired. I wasn't given a choice. Sad, but true.

---

*WHERE WERE THE CONDOMS?* I PROMISED YOU honesty, right? I said I wrote what I recalled, not a work of fiction.

Here's the truth: I was a complete and total moron, incapable of respecting HIV and its deadliness—or respecting myself enough to use protection. I knew better. Claiming ignorance was an excuse. The truth was that I didn't like condoms and made the moronic choice not to use them. You see how that turned out in this last book. Kids, don't be like Mike. Wrap that puppy. Pee-pee balloons are your friends.

---

*WHY DIDN'T YOU KEEP THE SERIES LIGHT AND FUNNY?* So many people have asked me this. I had a blast writing the first two books, laughing along with the characters as they said and did ridiculous things. But do you remember my promise to keep things real, to stick to what happened? Life wasn't always funny. Sometimes it hurt or sucked, or both—and I don't mean sucking in the fun, tingly way either. Breakups are hard. Lord knows I experienced enough of them. A piece of me died each time I lost someone I loved (Carter's kids in particular), but that was life. In order to keep the series consistent and take you through the real life of one main character, you had to experience it all. These were deliberate choices, and I don't apologize for them.

As with life, there will *always* be more humor and laughter. I promise—it gets better. Keep your chin up.

*WAS HEATH REALLY YOUR LAST DATE, AS THE TITLE states?* As of the writing of this book, Heath and I have been together for over eleven years. We've traveled the US playing tennis tournaments together, vacationed in Europe and the Mediterranean, and taken cruises throughout the Caribbean. We are truly blessed.

We were officially married at the end of November 2020. We live in Florida with our two Australian shepherds and old-man cattle dog, Cooper. Heath took me off the market for good.

---

To ALL THOSE FRUSTRATED BY THE BREAKUPS AND repeated HFNs (Happy For Now, to the uninitiated) in the previous books, Heath is my real-life Happily Ever After.

I love him with all my heart.

You're welcome, and thanks for waiting for him, like I did. 😊

*Casey*

# WHAT'S NEXT?

If you loved My Last Date, please take a moment to leave a review filled with stars. Your feedback fuels indie authors.

Let's stay in touch! Join the Casey Morales community & receive free ebooks, advance notice of releases, and other fun stuff!

We can also stay in touch online: My Website, Facebook, Instagram, Bookbub.

# ALSO BY CASEY MORALES

My Accidental First Date

My Next Date

My Wildest Date

My Dream Date

My Last Date